The BELIEVERS

by REBECCA C. JONES

BULLSEYE BOOKS

ALFRED A. KNOPF • NEW YORK

CHAPTER 1

IT WAS almost three o'clock, and Mrs. Crawley looked like she might drop any minute. But she pumped herself up for the final attack of the day.

"Boys and girls," she said, "we have a *wonderful* opportunity to help our school."

Lord, Tibby thought. Not another fund-raiser.

But it was. This time they weren't supposed to sell candy or cookies or Christmas cards. This time they were supposed to hustle pretzels. *Wonderful* pretzels, Mrs. Crawley said. Of the finest quality.

"And look," Mrs. Crawley said, holding up a tin can with a decorated lid. "Look at the nice tins these pretzels come in. This is a *real* copy of a *real* Currier and Ives print."

Lord. Would the excitement never stop?

"Can anyone guess what the proceeds of the pretzel sale will be used for?" Mrs. Crawley asked.

She folded her hands across her enormous belly and looked around the room. Back in October, when Tibby first came to St. Agnes, she thought Mrs. Crawley was pregnant because her arms and legs looked okay, but her stomach was huge. Even her clothes looked like they came from the Soon-To-Be Shop in the mall. But here it was, May already, and no sign of a little Crawley yet. Tibby guessed it was just fat.

"Well?" Mrs. Crawley said again. "Doesn't anyone want to take a guess?"

Sara Pifer, sitting up in the front row in her pressed uniform and polished oxfords, raised her hand.

"Yes, dear?" Mrs. Crawley smiled on Sara.

"Will the money be used for new audio-visual equipment?" Sara asked.

Mrs. Crawley shook her head but still beamed at Sara.

Sara tried again. "For new computers?"

"No, dear."

"Playground equipment?"

"Huh-uh." Tibby could tell Mrs. Crawley was enjoying this little game.

But Sara wasn't. She was used to being right, and now, after three wrong guesses, she was beginning to sound desperate.

"Library books? Art supplies? Musical instruments? Desks?"

Mrs. Crawley kept shaking her head. "I'll give

you a hint," she said. "The school hopes to raise five thousand dollars. Now what do you think would cost five thousand dollars?"

Lord. Tibby couldn't resist. She raised her hand.

Mrs. Crawley pretended not to notice Tibby. She concentrated on Sara. "Think very hard," she urged.

But Sara just sat there. She wasn't going to take a chance at being wrong again.

Tibby began waving her arm. A couple of kids looked at her and grinned. She couldn't disappoint them.

"I know what costs five thousand dollars," Tibby said out loud.

Mrs. Crawley couldn't ignore her now. "What, Tibelda?"

"Your grocery bill."

Sister Josephine, whose face always looked like she'd just taken a swig of pickle juice, pecked out the Parent Awareness Report on her old manual typewriter.

Name: Tibelda Taylor
Grade: 6-B
Reason for Parental Notification: Continued disrespect for classroom teacher.

 Sister Mary Josephine, SSND
 Vice Principal
 St. Agnes Elementary School

If you have any questions about the above problem, please call the school. Otherwise, sign one (1) copy of this report and have your child return it to school.

Tibby took the Parent Awareness Report from Sister Josephine and put it in her notebook carefully. She had to return one copy to school, but she could keep the original, and she didn't want it to get crumpled, like the last one. Tibby wanted all of her Parent Awareness Reports to be nice and smooth so someday she could wallpaper her bathroom with them. She planned to paste the black-and-white forms on the wall, then spray a shiny shellac over them all. It would look striking, especially with a red shower curtain.

"Tibelda, Tibelda, Tibelda." Sister Josephine wagged her head. "Sometimes I think you enjoy getting these Parent Awareness Reports."

Tibby tried not to grin.

The old nun sighed. "Why do you think your mother sends you to St. Agnes, Tibelda?"

That was an interesting question.

"She wants you to get a good Christian education, that's why."

No, that wasn't it. Tibby knew Veronica didn't give a hoot about Christian education. Veronica never went to church, and she said Tibby didn't have to go, either. Tibby was probably the only kid at St. Agnes who had never, ever been to Sunday Mass. She was proud of that fact.

Sister Josephine talked on and on — about Christian values and respect for authority and the importance of pretzel sales — but Tibby didn't listen. She was still considering that first question: Why *did* Veronica send her to St. Agnes?

Maybe Veronica sent her there because of a story she had done last year about Catholic schools and test scores. Veronica was a reporter, and she often made decisions based on stories she had covered.

Or maybe Veronica sent her to St. Agnes simply because that's where she herself went to school when she was a kid. Yes, that was it. Veronica wanted Tibby to grow up just like her — to become a beautiful reporter laughing under the television lights.

And if Tibby had to put up with fat teachers and pickle-faced nuns in order to do that, well, it was worth it.

CHAPTER 2

BY THE time Sister Josephine let Tibby go, the school parking lot was empty except for the old Buick that belonged to the nuns. Even Mrs. Mendelson had gone home.

Mrs. Mendelson was the third-grade teacher who stood at the edge of the playground every day and screeched at anybody who tried to take the shortcut through the woods by the river. "Don't go back there!" she always yelled. "There are drunks and perverts back there!"

Everyone at St. Agnes knew that Tibby Taylor took the forbidden shortcut whenever Mrs. Mendelson wasn't looking — and sometimes when she was. She took it every morning, even when it was muddy and the sidewalk would have been more convenient. And, of course, she took it whenever she stayed after school with Sister Josephine. Mrs. Mendelson might not be there, but a lot of St. Agnes kids lived in the neighborhood, and they would have seen her if she went on the sidewalk.

Tibby never saw a drunk or pervert on the wooded path, but she often said she did. There was one named Henry, she said, who offered her a nip every now and then. And there was another one, unnamed, who sometimes chased her and threatened to put his hand down her underpants. He made the best story.

The path ended at the scalloped brown fence that surrounded Tibby's yard. She had to watch carefully, climb the fence quietly, and go around front to enter the house. Aunt Evelyn didn't know she took the shortcut. Aunt Evelyn was the sort who might believe, and not enjoy, stories about drunks and perverts.

As Tibby came around the house today, she popped a piece of gum in her mouth. Aunt Evelyn didn't like chewing gum.

The old woman was waiting right inside the front door, smiling so wide that Tibby could see the gold in her back teeth. Aunt Evelyn always started out smiling.

"You're late," she said.

"I had to stop and get something."

"Oh? What?" Aunt Evelyn was probably trying to sound casual, but she didn't fool Tibby.

"It's a surprise," Tibby said. "For my mother."

"Oh." At the mention of Tibby's mother, Aunt Evelyn's gold-toothed smile faded. She had probably thought the surprise was for her.

"She's coming tomorrow, you know." Tibby smiled sweetly. "Do you need any help packing?" Aunt Evelyn always went back to her own house, where she belonged, when Veronica came home.

"Oh, Tibby." Tibby chomped harder on her gum, but her stomach still tightened. She knew, from the tone of Aunt Evelyn's voice, what was coming next. "I'm afraid Veronica won't be coming home tomorrow, Tibby."

"Why not?"

"Something has come up."

Something was always coming up.

Veronica Taylor worked for the network's Midwest bureau, so she had to go to a lot of dinky towns where crops had failed, or automobile-parts factories had shut down, or some kind of toxic waste was on the loose. Most of her stories went out on network feeds to local stations, but sometimes somebody in New York thought a story was important enough for the network's evening news. Then Veronica would call Tibby and say, "Did you see your mom on the boob tube tonight?"

And of course Tibby had. She never missed the evening news. She always watched for Veronica Taylor and spotted her, even when the camera showed nothing more than the back of her curly dark head as she asked one single (but amazingly insightful) question.

Tibby had answered one of those insightful questions herself once. It was a long time ago, so long that Tibby couldn't even remember the question. But she remembered the bright lights and the way Veronica had laughed at her answer. "I'd like to take this little sweetie home with me," Veronica had said when the lights were off and the interview was over. Those were her exact words, and that's exactly what she did, took Tibby home with her. She took her out of the foster home and adopted her as her very own. She didn't do it that day, of course, but pretty soon afterward.

So Tibby understood about her mother's work. It was important, the most important work in the world. And Veronica had to do it, even though she wanted, more than anything, to come home to her little sweetie.

Tibby knew how Veronica worried when she missed a trip home. She'd call to make sure Tibby was okay. So Tibby went upstairs to wait by the phone in her room.

Every time Tibby walked into her room, a little voice inside her gasped with pleasure. It was a beautiful room, just like one in a magazine, and almost everything in it was red. "That just proves she's my kid," Veronica had said when Tibby picked the color scheme. Veronica always surrounded herself with red: she wore red clothes, drove a red car, and lived in red rooms. "And now," she'd said, the day she took Tibby home, "I've even got a kid with red hair."

Tibby liked red, too, but that wasn't the best thing about her room. The best thing was all the gadgets in it. The computer, the television, the VCR, the telephone. Especially the telephone. It was red, and it was her own. Not like the one, a long time ago, at Mrs. Wilson's house. That one belonged to the telephone company, and when Mrs. Wilson didn't pay her bill, a man came and took it away. Then the social worker found out that Mrs. Wilson didn't have a phone, and she came and took Tibby away, too. It wasn't enough that Mrs. Wilson laughed a lot and sang "Take Me Out to the Ball Game" while she set Tibby's hair on pink spongy rollers. She didn't have a telephone, and that was all that mattered to the social worker.

But now Tibby had her own telephone. And she had her own mother, too, who was going to call her any minute.

The telephone rang, and Tibby jumped for it. But it wasn't Veronica. It was Patsy Franklin.

Patsy was a scrawny little kid who'd latched on to Tibby her first day at St. Agnes. She had allergies and blew her nose a lot, but she was a terrific judge of character. She thought most of the kids at St. Agnes were dull and boring, but Tibby, she said, had flair. Tibby liked having flair.

"Her grocery bill!" Patsy laughed. "That was

pretty good! I don't know how you think of them!"

"It's a gift," Tibby said.

Patsy laughed again. "What did Sister say?"

"She gave me another Parent Awareness Report."

"Which you'll sign yourself."

Tibby grinned. It was nice to have a reputation.

Then Patsy changed the subject. "Listen," she said, "my mom has to go out to the mall for some things, and she says you can come along. Want to?"

Tibby felt her flair being replaced by an ache, deep inside. It was an old, familiar ache, and Tibby knew just how to get rid of it.

"Sorry," she said. "My mom and I have some stuff to do."

"Really? I didn't know your mom was home. Do you think I can meet her this time?"

"We'll see," Tibby said.

The next time the phone rang, it really was Veronica, and — Tibby had been right — she was worried.

"Are you okay?" Veronica spoke in a soft voice, softer than the one she used on TV. "*Really* okay?"

"I'm fine."

"I'm sorry, Tib," Veronica said. "I must be the world's worst mother."

"No, you're not," Tibby assured her. "Just the busiest."

"You're a real trouper, you know, Tib?"

"Yeah." She waited. "Do you know when you *will* come home?"

"Oh, I don't know. This trial looks like it might *never* end."

"*Never?*"

"But when it's over, I'm going to take a nice long vacation," Veronica said, "so we'll have lots of time together. Maybe we can take a little trip somewhere. We'll go to Florida. Or Bermuda. Somewhere with a nice beach."

Tibby imagined herself running with Veronica into the waves. "That'll be great," she said.

"Won't it? We'll just lie on the beach and soak up the rays. We'll look like a couple of wrinkled old prunes by the time we leave, but who cares? We'll even — just a minute, Tib." Tibby heard muffled voices in the background. Then Veronica came back on the line. "Listen, Tib, I gotta go. Love ya!"

And, *click,* she was gone.

CHAPTER 3

AUNT Evelyn and Tibby always watched the news before dinner, but not together. Aunt Evelyn watched on the small black-and-white set in the kitchen, while she fixed dinner. Tibby watched by herself in her room with the door closed. That way when Veronica's face came on the screen, it was almost as if she were talking to Tibby alone, and nobody else.

But Veronica didn't come on tonight. Tibby wondered how a trial could be important enough to keep Veronica working — when she needed some time off so badly — but not important enough to make the national news.

Somebody in New York must be awfully stupid.

"No news is good news," Aunt Evelyn said, as she dished out the pot roast. That's what she always said when Veronica didn't have a spot on the news. Tibby knew she meant *well, at least she hasn't adopted another kid.*

Aunt Evelyn hadn't made any secret of the fact that she thought adopting Tibby was a mistake. "But you're not even married," she'd said when Veronica first brought Tibby to Seneca for a visit.

"So?" Veronica had said. "Lots of women raise children by themselves. And we won't have their financial problems."

"But there's more to motherhood than signing checks. And you're so busy. How will you ever manage?"

"Oh, we'll manage all right," Veronica had said, squeezing Tibby's shoulder. "Won't we, Tib?"

Tibby had nodded eagerly at her beautiful new mother — the one that was hers to keep — but Aunt Evelyn had just shaken her head. "Oh, Veronica," she'd said. "You just can't get so carried away with each and every story you cover."

"I don't," Veronica had said. "Just the important ones."

But there were so many important ones that sometimes even Tibby worried. Last summer, for instance, Veronica did a story about people moving back to their hometowns. It was one of those slow-paced pieces that the network ran on a Saturday evening. Everyone liked it a lot, and even Tibby thought it was one of the best stories her mother had ever done. She had no idea that Veronica would be inspired to trade their Chicago high-rise

16

for an old Victorian house just down the street from where she grew up.

"But what about the commute?" Aunt Evelyn had asked when she first heard of Veronica's plans. "It's a good two hours to Chicago."

"I'm hardly ever there anyway," Veronica had said, "and whenever I *am* home, it seems like I spend all my time looking for a new sitter. You know how hard it is to find good help in the city. Everyone's always looking for a better job. But here" — she looked out the window to the tree-lined street — "everything is so stable. And if a problem does come up, you'll be here to handle it. You don't mind, do you?"

Aunt Evelyn had sighed and said of course she didn't mind; she just wished Veronica would think things through a little better. But Tibby minded.

She missed those days of quitting sitters. She'd always looked forward to the frantic phone calls that brought Veronica home, sometimes for just half a day, to find a new sitter.

The first sitter in Seneca quit, too, but Aunt Evelyn didn't rush out and hire a new one the way Veronica had told her to. Instead, she packed her suitcase and moved into the guest room. She even brought her dog, a three-legged mongrel named Lou Grant.

"You don't have to move in," Tibby had told her, politely enough. "You're just supposed to find a new sitter."

"What, so she can up and quit, too?" Aunt Evelyn

had shaken her head. "Somebody has to stop this revolving door. Somebody has to take charge."

And, Lord, did Aunt Evelyn take charge. The very first morning she was there, she posted a schedule on the refrigerator. The schedule began with breakfast at 7:30 and ended with lights out at 9:30. The schedule allowed ninety minutes of free time every afternoon; otherwise, Tibby was supposed to march through a lockstep of school, homework, meals, and chores. The schedule said she had to make her bed every morning, load the dishwasher every other night, and empty the wastebaskets on Mondays and Thursdays.

If Tibby didn't do exactly what she was supposed to exactly when the schedule said she was supposed to do it, Aunt Evelyn would flash her silly gold-toothed smile and offer to help.

As if Tibby needed help emptying a wastebasket.

When Tibby told her mother about the schedule, Veronica laughed.

"Oh, Aunt E and her schedules!" Veronica said. "I bet she even schedules her trips to the bathroom!"

After that, Tibby did notice that the toilet in the hall bathroom flushed at the same time every morning.

Aunt Evelyn tried to slip Sunday Mass into Tibby's weekend schedule. But Tibby appealed to Veronica, long-distance, and this time her mother talked to the woman. With Tibby listening in on the extension, Veronica told Aunt Evelyn that Tibby could wait until she grew up to decide about God.

Aunt Evelyn didn't smile a bit about that. "A twig grows the way it's bent," she complained, but she didn't try to make Tibby go to church with her anymore. After all, Veronica was Tibby's mother, and she had the final say.

But tonight Aunt Evelyn was back to her gold-toothed smiling. Tibby had noticed before that the old woman was always extra cheerful whenever Veronica had to cancel a trip home. Lord, she was probably *glad* that Veronica had to work so hard and stay away so long; that way she could stay in charge.

After dinner Aunt Evelyn asked Tibby if she'd like to play Scrabble or gin rummy.

Tibby shook her head.

"Then how about going for a walk with Louie and me?" Aunt Evelyn reached down to scratch Lou Grant under the chin.

Lord. As if Tibby had nothing better to do than entertain wrinkly old ladies and their crippled dogs.

"I've got to do my homework," she said, virtuously. "It's on the schedule."

CHAPTER 4

TIBBY was taking the shortcut to school in the morning when she heard a voice say, "Oh, no."

Tibby's heart jumped to her throat. Was it a drunk? A pervert?

"Where's your mama?" the voice asked. It sounded like a kid. A sober, innocent kid. Tibby's heart settled back in her chest, and she walked ahead, around a bend in the path. There, kneeling on the ground, was a boy with red hair that stood out like bristles on a brush. He looked up.

"Oh, hi," he said. "I didn't know anyone else was here." Then he turned back to examining something on the path. Tibby looked over his shoulder and saw it was a tiny baby bird, so young that its creamy flesh hadn't sprouted feathers yet. It was cheeping softly, with its beak wide open.

"Do you know where this came from?" The boy's voice was almost accusing.

"No," Tibby said. "I just got here."

Gently, the boy picked up the bird and cradled it in his hand. "We'll have to find his nest and put him back." He seemed to assume Tibby would help.

"I thought you weren't supposed to touch baby birds," Tibby said.

"Who told you that?"

"*Everybody* knows the mother bird won't take care of a baby if someone's touched it," Tibby told him.

"Well, I guess you can mark that down as one more time *everybody's* wrong," he said, inspecting the branches of nearby bushes. "I've put lots of baby birds back in their nests, and their mothers always take care of them." He looked at Tibby. "Are you going to help or not?"

Tibby glanced down the path toward St. Agnes and thought of what Sister Josephine would say if she were late again. But if this kid wasn't going to worry about school, she wasn't about to dance off in any goody two shoes.

"Sure," she said. "I'll help."

They looked everywhere, up in the treetops, down in the bushes, even inside a hollow tree stump. But they couldn't find the nest. The bird's cheeping was getting even softer, and his beak was still open, begging for food.

"What should we do?" Tibby asked.

The boy looked worried. "Well, we could put the

21

bird on a high bush and hope his mother finds him."

"Do you think she will?"

He shook his head. "I think a cat'll find him. Or he'll starve to death. Baby birds have to eat constantly, and we don't know when this one was fed."

"We should feed him," Tibby said.

The boy shook his head again. "I've never been able to keep a bird this young alive. Older ones with feathers, yes, but never one this little."

"So what do you want to do?" Tibby asked. "Call a cat and offer him a snack?"

The boy looked at her and grinned. "I guess we could try."

"Good." Tibby turned to head back to her house. Maybe she could sneak in without Aunt Evelyn knowing.

"Where are you going?" the boy asked.

"Home. To get an eyedropper and some milk."

"What for?"

"To feed the bird." Lord, this kid was dumb.

"Is that something else everybody knows? That birds drink milk through an eyedropper?"

Tibby didn't say anything.

"They eat worms, mostly," he said.

"That thing can eat a worm?" The bird was hardly bigger than a worm, Tibby thought.

"Not just one worm," the boy said. "Lots of worms. And we'll have to chop them up." He watched her, and Tibby knew he was waiting to see how she liked the idea of chopping worms.

Tibby didn't flinch. "Where do we get the worms?" she asked.

The boy picked up a stick and tossed it to her. "Start digging," he said.

She used the stick to scrape at the ground for a few minutes. Then she tossed it aside and copied the boy, clawing at the cool earth with her bare hands.

The soil was soft from recent rains, and they found a lot of worms. The boy chopped them up with a stick and dropped small pieces, still wiggling, into the bird's open beak. The beak closed for barely a second as the bird swallowed, and then it was open again, begging for more.

"How much do we give him?" Tibby asked.

"Why?" the boy asked. "Do you want to quit?"

"No," Tibby said quickly. "I just wondered."

"He needs as much as we can give him," he said. "I've watched birds feed their babies constantly from sunrise to sunset. They stop just long enough to go get more worms."

They didn't talk anymore. They just kept digging and chopping and feeding. Off in the distance, Tibby heard St. Agnes' first bell, then its second. And she felt important, almost like one of those paramedics on TV, working to save a life. She dug faster.

The pile of worms grew faster than the little bird could eat. Tibby wondered if it still needed more, but she didn't ask. She didn't want the boy to think she was giving up.

And she didn't want to give up. She wanted this motherless bird to live and grow strong. Maybe someday he would fly, but never very far. He'd perch on her shoulder and perhaps nibble on her ear. She thought about giving him a name, but she didn't say anything because she didn't want the boy to think she was silly.

Suddenly the boy stopped digging. He sat up straight and looked at her. "Why aren't you in school?"

Tibby grinned at him knowingly. "Why aren't you?"

"I don't go to school."

Now it was Tibby's turn to sit up straight. "Not at all?"

"Oh, sometimes I go for a day or two. Just so the school officials will leave my parents alone. But you — "

Tibby didn't let him finish. "Do your parents know you don't go to school?"

"Sure," he said. "They don't want me to go. My father taught me to read the Bible, but he wants me — all of us — to stay away from the secular world."

"What's the secular world?" Tibby asked.

"People who aren't Believers." He looked at her. "But you belong in school."

"Just think of me as another believer."

He shook his head. "Your parents want you in school."

"Feed the bird," Tibby said. "His mouth is open."

The boy shook his head again. "Go to school."

"Then I'll feed him." Tibby reached for one of the chopped worms, but the boy put his hand over hers.

"Please don't let me lead you into sin," he said. "Go to school. Please."

Lead me into sin! Tibby started to laugh, but something in his eyes stopped her. "Oh, all right," she said. "I'll go to school. But don't forget to feed Taylor."

"Taylor?"

She nodded toward the bird. "That's his name." She liked the idea of giving the family name to the bird, the way Veronica had given it to her.

The boy grinned. "Taylor and I will be waiting for you after school, right here."

CHAPTER 5

TIBBY stopped by Sister Josephine's office after school to pick up another Parent Awareness Report. This one was marked *arrived at school late and in unkempt appearance.*

"I don't know what we're going to do with you, Tibelda," Sister said. "I know your mother's schedule makes a school conference practically impossible. And I don't think it would do any good to talk to a sitter" — she looked at the file from Tibby's old school — "especially when they seem to change so often." She shook her head. "This is a sad situation, very sad."

Tibby tried to look pitiful.

Sister sighed as she closed Tibby's folder. "But you have to learn to live by the rules, Tibelda. And you can start by checking your watch in the morning to make sure you arrive at school on time."

Tibby checked her watch right now and wondered how much longer this would take. She hoped the red-haired boy would wait.

He was waiting, all right, but he must have gone home sometime, because he had changed clothes since this morning. He was all dressed up in a stiff white shirt and a navy-blue tie, just like the boys at St. Agnes.

"I thought you said you didn't go to school," Tibby said.

"I don't. I have to help my father now."

"I thought you said you'd be able to take care of Taylor. All day." She looked around. "Where is he?"

"He died."

"What?"

"He died," the boy said again. "This morning, after you left."

"Why? What happened?"

The boy shrugged. "I told you I'd never been able to save one that young. He needed his mother."

She never should have trusted him. She should have stayed there and taken care of Taylor herself. With an eyedropper and some warm milk. Why had she listened to this kid with funny-looking hair? What made him an authority on baby birds? He was an authority on dead birds, that's what he was.

"But I can show you a whole nest full of baby birds," he said. "There are five of them, and the mother and father both — "

"What did you do with him?" Tibby demanded.

"Who?"

"Taylor. What did you do with him?"

"I put him in a compost pile."

"A compost pile!"

"Sure. That way his body'll rot and — "

"Rot!" That was the most disgusting thing she'd ever heard.

"I guess you don't want to see the nest."

What a smart kid.

Aunt Evelyn was waiting for her in the front hall again, with Lou Grant right beside her. The veins on her forehead stood out blue and bumpy, and she didn't even try one of her gold-toothed smiles. "All right," she said. "I want to hear your side of it."

"My side of what?"

"Why you can't follow the rules at St. Agnes. Why you were late for school this morning. And I'd especially like to know," she said, "what you've done with all the Parent Awareness Reports you were supposed to have brought home."

So Sister Josephine had decided to call the sitter after all.

"Well?" Aunt Evelyn said. "What do you have to say for yourself?"

"I'm saving the *Parent* Awareness Reports for my *parent*." Tibby smiled sweetly at her.

"For all intents and purposes, young lady, *I* am your parent."

Tibby stopped smiling. "And who," she asked, "is Veronica?"

"She's the one who got us into this situation."

Lord. As if Veronica wanted to stay away.

The doorbell rang. Lou Grant and Aunt Evelyn both started toward the door, but Tibby beat them. This was *her* house and *her* door. Hers and Veronica's.

She opened the door and saw the red-haired boy, still in his shirt and tie. With him was a short man with black hair, wearing a thin suit and carrying a Bible.

"Good afternoon, miss," the man said, smiling. "Is your mother or father home?"

"I am her aunt," said Aunt Evelyn, behind Tibby.

"She's just visiting," Tibby said.

He didn't seem to care. "Good afternoon, ma'am. Did you know the Lord God Almighty loves you?"

"I'm not interested," Aunt Evelyn said stiffly. "I'm Catholic."

The red-haired boy looked down at his shoes, but the man still smiled. "That's all right, ma'am. The Lord loves Catholics, too."

"I'm sorry," Aunt Evelyn said. "I'm not interested."

The man's mouth was open, ready to say more,

and the boy was looking up, into Tibby's eyes, when Aunt Evelyn shut the door.

"I hate to be rude," she said, more to herself than Tibby, "but if you're nice to these people, they never leave you alone."

She was probably right. Hadn't Tibby seen how the boy had pestered her into going to school?

"That boy looked like he recognized you," Aunt Evelyn said. "Do you know him?"

"Not really."

"Good."

Tibby wondered what would be wrong with knowing that boy. Whatever it was, it bothered Aunt Evelyn, and that was enough for her.

"Actually," she said, "he's a friend of mine. A very good friend."

"Really?" Aunt Evelyn looked doubtful.

"And I forgot to tell him something." Tibby ran outside and spotted the boy with his father, heading down the street. She wished, for Aunt Evelyn's sake, that she knew his name.

"Hey!" she shouted, and they both looked back. "Can I still see the bird's nest?"

The man looked puzzled, but the boy grinned. "Sure! I'll meet you on the path after school tomorrow."

"What path?" Aunt Evelyn asked when Tibby went back inside.

"Oh, it's just our usual meeting place."

Aunt Evelyn frowned.

"What's wrong?" Tibby asked sweetly.

"I'd like to know a little more about this boy before you get too involved."

"I'm pretty involved already," Tibby said, and she smiled, still sweetly, at the worried look that crossed Aunt Evelyn's face.

CHAPTER 6

TIBBY was in her seat before the first bell rang the next morning. She didn't raise her hand to say anything smart all day. And, when Sara Pifer passed around her autograph book at noon, Tibby just signed her name.

Patsy Franklin looked at Tibby's name in the book.

"Tibby Taylor?" Patsy said. "That's all?"

Tibby nodded.

"What's wrong? Are you sick or something?"

"I'm okay."

Patsy eyed her carefully. "You're up to something. You want to make sure you don't have to stay after school because you've got something planned for this afternoon. That's it, isn't it?"

Tibby just smiled, and Patsy laughed in that way that made Tibby feel so full of flair.

*　　*　　*

With Mrs. Mendelson watching, Tibby took the sidewalk home from school. She hurried to change her clothes and remind Aunt Evelyn that she was going to meet her very good friend, the red-haired boy whose father peddled Bibles door-to-door.

Aunt Evelyn stood at the door of Tibby's room and watched her snap her jeans. "What do you two do together?" she asked.

"Lots of things," Tibby said. "Yesterday we fed some worms to a baby bird."

"Oh." Aunt Evelyn looked relieved.

"But he's got something different planned for today."

The boy was waiting for her on the path, right where they'd dug for worms the day before. With him was a little girl, about six or seven years old. She had red hair, too, only it was long and held away from her face by a row of crossed bobby pins.

"This is Esther," he said. "She's my sister. And I'm Verl. Verl Milner."

"I'm Tibby Taylor."

"Taylor." He grinned. "Like the bird."

Esther looked at her as if she'd never seen another kid before.

"What's with her?" Tibby asked, and Verl shrugged.

"I like the way you're dressed," Esther said, in a squeaky voice. "Like a Barbie doll."

Tibby looked down at her jeans and red T-shirt.

They didn't look much like Barbie clothes to her, but she could see why they did to Esther. The kid was wearing a faded blue dress with a ragged collar and empty belt loops. The empty belt loops reminded Tibby of a dress she'd had when she was little, before Veronica.

"I can't stay long," she told Verl. "Where's the bird's nest?"

He nodded down the path, in the direction of St. Agnes. "Not far."

Good. She didn't want to spend too much time with these weird kids and their empty belt loops.

They followed the path to St. Agnes, then took the winding river road past the big old houses around the school. This was farther than Tibby had expected.

"Where is this nest?" she asked again.

"At Solimano's lot," Esther said. "Where the Indians used to live."

"How far is it?"

"Not far," Verl said again.

They didn't say anything else. At least these kids didn't yak and say dumb stuff just to fill the air.

As they followed the river road, the houses grew smaller, but the spaces between them grew. They passed a barn, set back from the road and painted a bright yellow.

"That's ours," Esther said proudly. "That's where we praise the Lord."

"In a barn?" Tibby looked at Verl, but he didn't say anything.

34

"Sure," Esther said. "It's real nice inside, especially when everybody sings."

"Good Lord," Tibby said.

"Praise His holy name," Esther said.

Tibby looked at her, then back at Verl.

"You forgot to say it, Verl," Esther squeaked.

But Verl ignored her. He pointed to a small brick ranch house ahead. "That's where Mr. Solimano lives," he said, "and the Indian campground is back there." He pointed to a big empty lot with a circular flower bed flanked by white blossoming trees.

"What makes you think Indians lived in a place like that?" Tibby asked. She'd always thought Indians lived in dusty places, on reservations.

"Mr. Solimano said so," Esther said, as if that ought to convince anybody of anything.

"And I've found some stuff back there," Verl said.

"What kind of stuff?"

"Arrowheads, mostly," Verl said. "C'mon, I'll show you. But first I have to let him know we're here." He led them around the house to a back door. Verl rang the bell, and a big, heavy man with weathered skin and white hair came to the door.

"Good afternoon, Mr. Solimano." Verl sounded just like his father when he'd brought the Bible to Tibby's door.

"Well, hello there!" Mr. Solimano's booming voice reminded Tibby of the Santas that sell cars and furniture on TV every Christmas. "I didn't think you were coming today. And bringing Esther, too." He smiled at the little girl, and she grinned back.

"I'm not here to work, sir. I brought my friend Tibby to see the place."

"It's a real pleasure to meet you, Tibby." Mr. Solimano stuck out his hand, and Tibby shook it.

"Would it be all right if I showed her around the campground, sir? There's a bird's nest I'd like her to see."

Tibby thought Verl was laying on the sirs pretty thick, but Mr. Solimano lapped it up. "Of course it would!" He winked at Tibby. "Verl goes back to that campground so often that I think he's on a first-name basis with some of the old chiefs."

"Thank you, sir."

"Any time, Verl, any time." And he shut the door.

"He's a nice man," Esther said as they walked away.

"The nicest I've ever worked for," Verl said, and Tibby looked at him. He looked about her age, maybe a little bit older, but he talked like somebody who'd held dozens of jobs.

"What do you do for him?" she asked.

"Yard work, mostly. There's a lot to do."

Tibby didn't know much about yard work, but she knew grass like this didn't grow naturally. It was smooth and even, almost like a carpet. And the circular garden they passed had no weeds. Just evenly spaced purple and white flowers, with wood chips covering the ground between them.

They walked up a gentle slope that Tibby hadn't noticed from the street. Big old trees replaced the blossoming ornaments below. Then, at the top of the hill, the clipped grass stopped. From then on, it was wild, with patches of soft spring flowers poking through the underbrush between the trees.

"There's a path to the river over here," Verl said, leading the way. "Mr. Solimano figures the Indians lived down near the water. They probably kept lookouts at the top of the hill."

Verl took long sideways steps down the narrow dirt path. Tibby and Esther tried to do the same, but the path was pretty steep, and they almost ran down the hill. They bumped into Verl when he stopped in front of them.

"There," he said, pointing to a tree downhill in front of them. "Can you see the nest?"

Tibby followed his finger with her eyes, but all she could see was a tangle of leaves and branches.

"I don't see it," Esther said.

"Right there." Verl kept pointing.

"I see it! I see it!" Esther cried.

"Hush," Verl said. "You'll scare them."

Tibby still didn't see the nest, but she didn't want to admit it.

"Do you see the dead branch, with no leaves on it?" Verl asked. "Right above that."

Tibby was just about to say she saw it, just so he'd leave her alone, when she really did see it. A brown nest with four — no, five open beaks. The heads were bigger than Taylor's, and they were sprouting a light brown fuzz.

"Good Lord," Tibby breathed.

"Praise His holy name," Esther said.

"How old do you think they are?" Tibby asked.

"About a week. Maybe ten days."

"You forgot to praise His holy name," Esther told Verl.

"Hush," Verl said. "We're making too much noise, and it's probably keeping the mother away. Let's go down to the river."

He led them down the path to a place where the river bent. A finger-shaped piece of land jutted out to form a little peninsula that trapped water in a small glasslike pond, undisturbed by the rushing river. Verl picked up a stone and threw it so it skipped four times over the water before disappearing.

Tibby wondered how he did that.

"You need a flat stone," Verl said. "Then you throw sideways, like this." He threw another, and it skipped five times.

Tibby found a flat stone and threw it *plunk* into the water. She tried another, and it *plunk*ed, too.

Verl found another flat stone for her. "It just takes practice," he said, "and remember to flick your wrist sideways."

She wanted to tell him not to bother, that she wasn't the athletic type. But she tried it once more, this time flicking her wrist sideways, and the stone skipped twice before sinking.

"Good Lord!" she cried. "I did it!"

"Praise His holy name," Esther said, and looked pointedly at Verl.

"Why do you keep saying that?" Tibby asked.

"I praise His holy name night and day," Esther chanted, then added with a smile, "so I can get a Barbie doll."

"A Barbie doll!" Tibby hooted.

"And maybe a Ken, too."

"You think God gives stuff to people just because they run around praising his name?" Tibby said.

"Sure, He does! Doesn't He, Verl?"

They both looked at him. "Well . . . ," he began.

"Sister Roberta praised His holy name, and she got a new washing machine. And Brother Michael praised His holy name, and he got a new car." Esther folded her arms, satisfied. "I figure my Barbie doll will be showing up any day now."

"How do you know those people got all that stuff?"

"They said so at meeting. Didn't they, Verl?"

Verl nodded, then headed up the path. "C'mon," he said, "I'll show you the arrowheads."

But Tibby held back. "Why don't you just ask your parents for a Barbie doll?"

"Papa says we shouldn't waste money on worldly pleasures. He says we should give our money over to the Lord's work."

"And the Lord's work is getting you a Barbie doll?" Tibby laughed.

"If the Lord wants us to have something, He'll see that we get it," Esther said.

"Good Lord," Tibby said, just so she could hear the squeaky reply:

"Praise His holy name."

CHAPTER 7

THEY followed the path, past the tree with the nest in it, to a small clearing where several rocks had been shoved together to form a crude box. Verl reached in and pulled out three flat stones with pointed tips.

"These are arrowheads," he said, handing one to Tibby. "See how the stone's been chipped away to form a point?"

Tibby examined the stone. She could see small marks, smoothed by time, where the stone had been shaped into an arrow.

"Why do you keep them here?" She handed back the stone. "Why don't you take them home?"

"They belong to Mr. Solimano," he said.

"Then why doesn't he take them inside where they'll be safe?"

"He says they belong out here, where the Indians

left them," Verl said, "and I think he's right. But I pushed these rocks together to protect them. He said that would be okay."

Tibby didn't care what Mr. Solimano said. If she'd found the arrowheads, she would have taken them home.

Verl reached into the rock box again and pulled out something wrapped in an old checkered shirt. "Here's the prize," he said as he carefully unwrapped what looked to Tibby like an old dog bone. "I found it near some rocks down by the water, and at first I thought it was an old bone, but look, it's made of wood, and something's been carved on it."

"What is it?" Tibby asked.

He shrugged. "I don't know. And neither does Mr. Solimano."

Tibby took the piece of wood and ran her fingers over the marks. "Lord," she said.

"Praise His holy name," Esther squeaked.

"Hush now, Esther." Verl turned to Tibby. "I wish you'd quit doing that."

"Quit doing what?"

"Taking the Lord's name in vain," Verl said. "I think you're doing it on purpose, just to get Esther riled."

Actually, the word had just slipped out, without Tibby thinking. But this kid didn't need to get so high and mighty.

"I'm just doing her a favor," Tibby said sweetly.

"I figure, the more name-praising she does, the sooner she'll get her Barbie."

"Oh, thank you, Tibby," Esther said softly.

Tibby smiled at her. "You're Lord God Almighty welcome."

"Praise His holy name!"

Verl reached for the carved stick in Tibby's hand. "Give it back," he said.

Tibby held the stick away from him. "Why?" she asked. "What'd I do?"

"Give it back," he repeated quietly, "and stop your teasing."

Talk about a kid with no flair. She tossed back his old dog bone. And that's probably all it was, an old dog bone with teeth marks on it.

Aunt Evelyn was waiting for her. "I'm glad you're home," she said. "I think we need to have a talk."

Now what?

"I've done some checking on your friend and his family. They belong to that group that meets in the old Jackson barn."

"So?"

"So that's a very dangerous group, Tibby. Their leader has brainwashed them into thinking they don't need schools or doctors or anything. They think God will take care of everything."

Even getting a Barbie doll, Tibby thought, and she smiled.

"It's not funny, Tibby. People could die simply because they refuse to call a doctor. They think they can pray their way through anything."

"A lot of people pray."

"Yes, but they pray while they call the doctor. The Lord helps those who help themselves, I always say."

Tibby didn't argue. Why should she defend those weird kids with their old dog bones and empty belt loops? She should just forget about them.

She went up to her room and dialed Patsy's number. She needed to feel a little flair.

But Patsy's brother said she'd gone to the mall again with her mom. Tibby hung up and looked out the window. She wondered what those weird kids were doing right now. Probably praising His holy name and watching the sky for Barbie dolls.

Wouldn't that be something, though, if you really could get things just by praying for them? Tibby knew just what she'd pray for.

She turned away from the window and flipped on the TV. A Hostess cupcake commercial was on, and a bunch of kids were crowding around a mother with a tray full of snacks. The mother looked sort of like Veronica, with dark hair and bright, smiling eyes. She put an easy arm around one of the kids, and Tibby knew that one was her daughter.

Tibby turned off the TV. Lord, she wished Veronica would come home. And put an easy arm around her.

44

Lord, send Veronica home. Please send her home. Praise His holy name and send Veronica home. Praise . . . Veronica . . . praise . . . Veronica.

"Tibby!" Aunt Evelyn called. "Veronica is on the phone."

It was a miracle!

"Tibby! Did you hear?"

"I hear!" *A miracle.* She picked up the phone in her room. "Hello?"

"Hi, Tib."

"Hi!"

"Aunt E says she's a little worried about you."

Don't worry about it. It's not important. Just come home.

"She says she thinks you're getting mixed up with some very strange people." Veronica pronounced *very strange* so it sounded like *vehly stlange*, and Tibby giggled.

"And she thinks you should spend some time with someone even stranger . . . me."

Veronica was coming home! Praise His holy name!

"But I can't come home right now. I have to go to Washington to finish a story I'm working on, so . . . "

Forget His holy name.

". . . I wondered if you'd like to fly and meet me there."

"In Washington?"

"I don't think it would hurt for you to miss a few days of school, do you?"

Tibby couldn't speak.

"Or do you have something planned?"

"No!"

"Then Aunt E will try to get plane tickets for Thursday, okay?"

Thursday. Just two more days. Praise His holy name!

Tibby found Verl and Esther walking away from Solimano's lot.

"It worked!" she said. "I praised His holy name, and I got what I wanted!"

"That fast?" Esther said. "You didn't have to wait a long time?"

"What did you pray for?" Verl asked.

"For my mother to come home. She's not coming home, but I'm going to see her. And that's even better!"

"Good." Verl grinned. "Very good."

"Where does your mother live?" Esther asked.

"She lives here, but she works — oh, never mind, it's too complicated to explain. The important thing is, this praising stuff really does work! I wouldn't be surprised if it started raining Barbie dolls right this very minute!"

Esther looked up to the sky. "Praise His holy name!" she shouted.

CHAPTER 8

WASHINGTON'S National Airport was crowded, and Tibby didn't see her mother right away. For a moment her stomach tightened with the thought that something else had come up and she would have to fly back to Aunt Evelyn. But then she saw her, smiling and waving.

In a moment, her mother's arms were around her, and Tibby sank into the sweet-smelling softness. She could have stayed there forever, but Veronica gently pulled away to look her over.

"My God, you've grown!" she said. "Every time I slip away for a few days, you shoot up another foot!"

"It's been almost three weeks this time." As soon as she said it, Tibby wanted to snatch back the words. She didn't mean to criticize.

But Veronica didn't seem to mind. "I know," she

said. "It's been a long time, much too long. We have a lot of catching up to do." She slipped an arm around Tibby's shoulders. "Let's go get your luggage."

Tibby felt like skipping down the concourse, but she kept perfect pace with her mother. Veronica must have noticed, because she gave her shoulder an extra squeeze.

"I bet you're glad to get a few days off," Veronica said. "I remember this is the time of year when school seems to go on and on."

Tibby nodded dumbly. She wished she could think of something clever and exciting to say. She didn't want Veronica to get bored.

"So what have you been up to lately?" Veronica asked.

Tibby tried to think of something interesting. "I went to see an old Indian campground the other day," she began, but that sounded boring, too.

"Really?" Veronica smiled her beautiful smile. "Then I bet you'd like to visit the Museum of Natural History here. They have lots of stuff about Indians."

"Oh, you don't have to take me there." Tibby didn't want to be any trouble.

"Actually, I was thinking it would be a fun place for you to go by yourself."

"By myself?"

"Yes." Veronica squeezed her shoulder again. "You could go there while I finish up one more interview this afternoon, and then we'll meet for dinner. Doesn't that sound like fun?"

"You have to work this afternoon?"

"Just a little bit. It won't take long."

Don't be stupid, Tibby told herself. Of course she has to work. If she didn't, she would have come home.

They took a taxi across a big bridge and past the dome-shaped Jefferson Memorial. Then they rode across a long green park that her mother called the Mall. She pointed out one window to the Capitol building, which looked much bigger than Tibby had expected, and out the other to the tall, pointed Washington Monument. A lot of white buildings lined the Mall, and Veronica seemed to know them all.

The taxi turned and stopped in front of one of the buildings. A sign said it was the Museum of Natural History.

"Here it is," Veronica said. "I'll keep your suitcase, and I'll meet you right in front here when the museum closes. Make sure you come out the Madison Drive exit, okay?" She gave Tibby another squeeze. "Have fun!"

Tibby wanted to stay in the car for more squeezes, but her mother gently nudged her out.

"Here, I almost forgot." Veronica reached out of the taxi to press a crisp bill into Tibby's hand. "Get something to eat and maybe something at the museum shop." Then Veronica blew her a kiss and was gone.

Tibby watched the taxi leave, then looked down at the money in her hand. It was a fifty-dollar bill.

The skeleton of a huge old elephant stood in the center of the museum's circular lobby. Beneath him, and around him everywhere, were kids — and grown-ups yelling at kids.

She saw the sign for the museum shop but decided to look around first. The first floor had more skeletons and lots of other dead stuff. Dead fish, dead birds, and all kinds of dead animals stuffed and behind glass so they looked real. Tibby remembered hearing once that Roy Rogers had stuffed his horse Trigger and put him in a museum somewhere. She looked for Trigger but didn't see him.

She was getting hungry, so she went down to the museum's snack bar for a hamburger and a Coke. The cashier looked up when Tibby handed her a fifty-dollar bill. She probably wasn't used to getting that much money from a kid, Tibby thought. Other kids don't have a mother like Veronica.

After lunch she went up to the Hall of Prehistoric North American Culture on the second floor. Life-size Indians stood and squatted in wooded scenes behind glass. The figures looked so real that Tibby wondered at first if they'd been shot and stuffed, like the animals downstairs. But she figured dead skin wouldn't look that fresh. They were probably made of wax.

But, Lord, they looked real. As if a camera had stopped their actions for just a fraction of a second. Tibby could almost hear them, talking softly, laughing, crying.

She moved on to exhibit cases of Indian relics. There were rows and rows of arrowheads, like the ones Verl had. And there were wooden spoons, snowshoes, beaded moccasins, lacrosse sticks, even a turtle-shell rattle for a baby.

Then she saw it. The prayer stick. That's what the museum called it, but it looked exactly like Verl's old dog bone. Only this one was cleaner. The label beneath it said the prayer stick was used at religious ceremonies by the Kickapoo Indians. The etched markings were supposed to remind them of prayers and past events.

Tibby was still looking at the prayer stick when a voice over the loudspeaker said the museum shop would close in fifteen minutes. She still had more than forty dollars.

She followed a pack of Boy Scouts down the wide stairs to the museum shop. It was crowded, especially around the T-shirts and postcards. She found a postcard of the Washington Monument for Patsy. She thought about getting one of an old skeleton for Aunt Evelyn, but decided not to.

Then she moved over to the book section. Veronica always liked books. If Tibby bought one, she'd probably say she knew she had the right kid again, like she did when Tibby picked red for her room.

She found a large paperback book with photographs of Indian relics. It even showed a prayer stick.

Then the voice came back on the loudspeaker and said the whole museum would close in another fifteen minutes. Lord, she'd better hurry. She took the book and pushed ahead of a pigtailed kid waiting in line at the cash register.

"Children without manners shouldn't be left alone in stores," Pigtail's mother said, loud enough for everyone to hear.

But Tibby didn't care. She had to hurry, or she'd be late for Veronica.

CHAPTER 9

TIBBY had to wait outside the museum for a few minutes, but she didn't mind. It gave her time to think about the coming night.

They didn't have to do anything fancy. They could just stay in their hotel and watch TV. Tibby remembered snuggling with Veronica in front of the TV once, right after the adoption. Veronica made popcorn that night, and they both threw kernels at the bad guys when they came on the screen. Lord, Tibby had laughed.

Or maybe they would eat at a hot dog stand and walk around town, looking at closed shop windows and planning what they'd buy someday. She did that with Mrs. Wilson once. They might even go to a mall, the way Patsy and her mother always did.

Then she saw Veronica hurrying across the street toward her.

"Whew!" Veronica was out of breath. "We got stuck in traffic, and I didn't want to be late, so we parked the car, and . . ."

But Tibby was staring at the tall, sandy-haired man who had just caught up with them.

"Oh, I'm sorry," Veronica said. "Larry, this is my daughter, Tibby. Tibby, this is Larry Speitel. He's one of those rare people who actually grew up in Washington, and he's offered to show us around tonight."

Larry grinned. "Tibby," he said. "What an unusual name."

Tibby didn't say anything. Who was this guy? And when was he going to leave?

"Her real name is Tibelda," Veronica said.

"Tibelda! Good grief, Veronica, where'd you come up with a name like that?"

"I didn't. That's the name she came with. It was part of the package." Veronica put a hand on Tibby's shoulder and gave it a little squeeze. "Right, Tib?"

Tibby nodded.

"You mean you adopted her? How old was she? Were you married?"

It's none of his business, Tibby thought. Don't answer him.

But Veronica just laughed. "Yes. Eight. And no."

Larry whistled softly. "My word, Veronica. And I thought you were just another pretty face."

She laughed again. "Come on, Larry. Are we going to eat, or aren't we?"

Larry held out his arm, and Veronica took it. Tibby walked behind them, her stomach tightening.

They ate in a glass-enclosed restaurant overlooking the Potomac River. Larry and Veronica each ordered a seafood platter, but Tibby asked for steak. With steak, you knew what you were getting.

Larry and Veronica talked for a little while about the view, and about some senator that Veronica had interviewed that day. Then Larry turned to Tibby. "So, Tibby, what grade are you in?" He spoke very distinctly, as if Tibby didn't understand English.

"Sixth," Tibby said, just as distinctly.

He nodded. "And, uh, do you go to a public school, private school, or what?"

"I go to a Catholic school."

"Good grief, Veronica, you send your kid to the nuns?"

Her mother laughed. "It's the same school I went to when I was a kid."

"Oh, God." Larry turned to Tibby. "And I bet she's got you in her old Girl Scout troop or something cute like that?"

"Excuse me," Tibby said. "I think I'm going to throw up."

She went to the ladies' room and locked herself in a stall. Her stomach really did hurt.

A few minutes later, Veronica knocked on the door. "Are you okay?" she asked. "Can I do anything?"

Get rid of that jerk, Tibby wanted to say, but she thought better of it. What if Veronica really liked this guy? What if she felt like she had to choose between him and Tibby? Which one would she choose?

"I'm okay," Tibby said. "I'll be out in a minute."

After dinner Larry drove them around to see the white government buildings, glistening under spotlights against the night sky.

"It's beautiful, just beautiful," Veronica kept saying.

"Kind of takes your breath away, doesn't it?" Larry said. But Tibby noticed he wasn't looking at a building when he said that. He was looking at Veronica's face.

They were rounding the Lincoln Memorial when Veronica asked if they could stop and get out. "I'd like Tibby to see this," she said.

Larry found a parking space, and they crossed the street to the memorial. Tibby meant to stay with them, but Larry and Veronica went too slowly up the enormous staircase, and Tibby felt uneasy without a railing. She hurried on ahead.

A gigantic statue of Abraham Lincoln sat in the memorial. As big as it was, the statue looked real, as if Lincoln himself were looking down on Tibby. His face looked sad, and kind.

"Every time I come here, this place gives me the

chills," Larry was saying, right behind her. "It's as if old Abe himself is . . ."

But Tibby didn't want to hear what Larry thought old Abe was doing. She went outside and sat on the top step, in the shadows. She waited there a long time, looking down the Mall to the Washington Monument, and to the Capitol beyond that.

How long was this guy going to hang around? Why did Veronica put up with him? Was he that important to her? More important than Tibby?

She looked back, over her shoulder, at Abraham Lincoln. He looked so gentle, so understanding, that for a moment she thought about climbing up one of his huge legs, onto his lap. But that lap would be cold and hard. It was no place to snuggle.

Please give me some time with Veronica, all alone. Praise His holy name. Some time alone.

Finally Larry and Veronica came out.

"Can you imagine?" Veronica was saying. "Thirteen years old, on drugs, and pregnant. She never had a chance."

"What happened to her?"

Tibby didn't want Larry to hear this story, but she could never move when it was being told.

"She died four years later. An overdose. That's when Tibby went to her first foster home."

"Her first? How many did she go to?"

"I'm not sure. Four or five, I think."

"Good grief. Then you found her. What a — "

Tibby stood up and stepped out of the shadows. "Are you ready to go?"

"Sure." Larry's voice dripped with pity. "Where do you want to go now? The Vietnam Memorial?"

Veronica shook her head. "It's getting late, and I've got an early day tomorrow," she said. "I think you'd better drop us off at the hotel."

Praise His holy name.

Veronica sat on the edge of the bed and stroked Tibby's hair away from her face. "I wish we could spend more time like this, just you and I," she said. "And someday we will. Someday" — she looked out the window next to Tibby's bed — "I'll get assigned to the Washington bureau, and I won't have to travel so much. We'll buy a house, maybe in Virginia, and I'll come home every night."

A warm tingle rushed through Tibby's body, and she wanted to follow Veronica's gaze out the window to that home in Virginia. But first she had to find out.

"How important is Larry?" she asked.

"Oh, I'd say he's an upper-middle-level bureaucrat."

"No, I mean how important is he to *you*?"

"To me?" Veronica laughed and looked back at Tibby again. "Is that what you've been stewing about all night?" She tucked the covers under Tibby's chin. "I just met him yesterday, and you don't need to worry. I have no intention of running off to Tahiti with him."

The warm tingle rushed back. Lord, she'd been silly. Nothing could come between Veronica and her little sweetie.

CHAPTER 10

T IBBY went to the Air and Space Museum while Veronica worked the next day. Tibby still had more than twenty-five dollars, and she spent it on lunch and a colorful Thai dragon kite. Tibby had never flown a kite, but she'd seen several sailing over the Mall. This one had a twenty-foot tail, and Tibby could just imagine Veronica laughing and running with her to get it up in the air. She bought plenty of string so it could soar, maybe as high as the Washington Monument.

Tibby went outside when the museum closed, just as she had the day before. She didn't see her mother right away, but she wasn't worried. It was Friday afternoon, and the traffic was probably even worse than the day before.

Cars and bikes clogged the street in front of her, and the sidewalk was crowded with people. Some of them were families with street maps and cameras. Others were office workers in three-piece suits and chunk heels. Tibby searched them all for Veronica's face.

She waited a long time — so long that the crowds began to thin, and even the traffic began to clear a little. A patrol car passed her a couple of times — Tibby thought it was the same one — and then it pulled over. A policeman leaned out the window and asked if she was lost.

"No," Tibby said. "I'm waiting for my mother."

But where was she?

Maybe she couldn't get a cab. Maybe she forgot where they were supposed to meet. Or maybe she'd been in an accident. What if Veronica had been hurt? Or killed?

Tibby shook off those frightening thoughts. She just had to wait.

Please let Veronica come. Praise His holy name. Let Veronica come. Praise . . . Veronica . . . praise . . . Veronica.

The sunlight was fading and the streetlights were just coming on when the cab pulled up. Veronica jumped out.

"Oh, Tib, I'm so sorry!" she cried. "I was in an editing booth and had no idea what time it was. How can you ever forgive me?"

"It's okay," Tibby said. And with Veronica's arms around her, it really was.

"Look," Veronica said, once they were in the cab, "I got something for us when I was out today."

61

"I got something, too," Tibby said.

"Open mine first," Veronica said.

Tibby opened the package. It was a game, called a Ouija board.

"I used to have one of these when I was a kid," Veronica said. "It was terrific at slumber parties. I thought we could use it tonight, as part of our celebration."

"What are we celebrating?"

Veronica smiled her beautiful smile. "The good times we've had together. How happy I am that you came. How I wish we could stay longer."

Tibby's stomach tightened. "We're leaving?"

"Some terrible tornadoes have ripped through the Midwest, and they're expecting more. I have to be in Fort Wayne in the morning."

"But I thought you were coming home after this story. For a vacation."

Veronica's smile faded. "Oh, I wish I could, Tib. I really do. But some people have *died*. Others have lost their homes. I just can't think about a vacation now."

Tibby understood and felt ashamed for thinking of a vacation at a time like this. "Can I come with you?"

"I wish you could, Tib. But there'd be nothing for you to do and nowhere for you to stay."

"I could stay with you."

Veronica shook her head. "I've been to these disaster areas before, and every cot — every corner — is taken."

"But there'll still be room for you?"

"Not really, but I *have* to be there."

Tibby understood that, too. If Veronica didn't go, how would the world ever find out what had happened? But understanding didn't make her feel better. She rubbed her stomach and hoped she wouldn't throw up.

Veronica smiled. "So what did you buy today?" she asked.

Tibby's throat was too full to answer. She held out her package, and Veronica opened it.

"A dragon kite! That's great! And I bet Aunt E will know a good place to fly it."

All during dinner a silent clock was ticking inside Tibby. Veronica said they'd go to the airport together in the morning. Her flight to Fort Wayne would leave first, at 7:55, and Tibby's would leave forty minutes later. That meant they had eleven hours together. Ten hours and fifty-five minutes. Ten hours and fifty minutes.

Two women at the next table kept looking at Veronica.

"They recognize you," Tibby said.

Veronica looked at them, smiled, and nodded. "No, they don't," she said. "I look familiar, but they can't figure out who I am. But give me time, Tib, give me time. Time and the right story. Then they won't wonder who I am. They'll *know*." A hard look came into her eyes that Tibby had never seen before.

Then, as quickly as it came, the look vanished, and Veronica was smiling her beautiful smile again. "So you've never played with a Ouija board before?" she asked.

"I don't even know what a Ouija board is," Tibby said.

"It's a game where the spirits talk to you and tell you about the future." Veronica lowered her voice. "It's *vehly* spooky."

"What kind of spirits? Do they talk out loud?"

Veronica tweaked a make-believe mustache. "Vee shall see, my dear, vee shall see."

Tibby laughed, but the clock inside her kept right on ticking.

With the clock ticking in Tibby's head, she didn't really feel like playing a game. She'd rather just sit, close to her mother, and talk about what they'd do after Veronica finished the story in Fort Wayne. If they picked a place for their vacation now, maybe Tibby could get information about it. She might even be able to make reservations. And, after the vacation, maybe Tibby could go to Veronica's next assignment with her. Maybe they'd be a team, and travel around the world — or at least the Midwest — together.

But Veronica was set on playing with the Ouija board, and Tibby didn't want to disappoint her. So they turned off the lamps in their hotel room, leaving only a thin streak of light from the bathroom. Then they pulled two chairs together so they sat facing each other, with their knees touching and the Ouija board across their laps.

The Ouija board was small, compared to most board games, and it had the words YES and NO written at the top. In the center, surrounded by scrollwork, were numbers and letters.

Veronica placed a small wooden triangle on top of the Ouija board. "The spirits use this pointer to send us messages," she said. "Rest your fingers on it lightly."

They both put their fingertips on the pointer.

"You're too tense," Veronica said. "Try to relax and open your mind."

Tibby slumped a little in her chair and hoped that counted as relaxing. The pointer began to move.

It moved slowly at first in small circles, then more quickly in wider ones.

"Do you know who we are?" Veronica asked in a low voice.

The pointer circled to the word YES.

"Who are we?"

The pointer circled to T-A-I-L-O-R-S.

"Lousy speller," Veronica grumbled. Then in her low, spooky voice, she said, "Tell us, great spirit, what will become of Tibelda Taylor when she grows up?"

The pointer circled to R-I-C-H-A-N-D-F-A-M-O-U-S.

Rich and famous. Tibby grinned. "Are you pushing it?" she asked.

"Would I do something like that?" Veronica asked, and Tibby knew she was.

Veronica lowered her voice again. "And what will become of Veronica Taylor?"

F-A-T-A-N-D-U-G-L-Y.

"I beg your pardon!" Veronica sniffed, and Tibby laughed. She couldn't imagine her mother being fat and ugly.

"And what about Aunt E?" Veronica asked.

D-E-A-D . . .

Lord. Tibby's fingers slipped off the pointer, but it went on, with just Veronica.

. . . L-Y-S-E-R-I-O-U-S.

Oh. Deadly serious. That was okay. Tibby put her fingers back on the pointer.

"Will I *ever* get assigned to the Washington bureau?" Veronica asked.

Tibby knew this was an important question, so she was pleased to see the pointer go straight, without circling, to YES.

"You're just trying to make up for fat and ugly," Veronica said. "But tell me, when will I get the Washington assignment?"

B-E-L-I-E-V-E.

"I do believe. I just want to know when."

So did Tibby. She wanted to know when Veronica wouldn't have to travel so much, when she would come home every night to that house in Virginia.

The pointer circled again to B-E-L-I-E-V-E.

"Let's try this one more time," Veronica said. "When will I be assigned to the Washington bureau?"

B-E-L-I-E-V-E.

"Oh, for crying out loud." Veronica sounded annoyed, and Tibby felt a chill on her spine. If Veronica was pushing the pointer — and she was, wasn't she — why didn't she make it answer her questions right?

"Looks like the spirits are getting tired," Veronica said. "Do you have any messages before you leave?"

The pointer shot over to YES.

"What is it?"

H-E-L-P.

"What?"

H-E-L-P-H-E-L-P-H-E-L-P.

"Who are we supposed to help?"

V.

Tibby expected the pointer to spell out the rest of Veronica's name. But the pointer didn't circle to another letter. It just stopped.

"Don't stop now," Veronica said. "Keep going."

The pointer sat there, on the V.

Veronica sighed and took her fingers off the pointer. "I guess the spirits have left."

H-E-L-P-H-E-L-P-H-E-L-P-H-E-L-P-V.

Even after the lights were out and Veronica's breathing was slow and regular with sleep, Tibby felt those letters rushing through her. H-E-L-P-H-E-L-P-H-E-L-P-H-E-L-P-V.

The Ouija board was just a game, Tibby told herself. And Veronica was pushing the pointer to make it spell words.

67

Then why didn't it spell what Veronica wanted? And why did it stop?

No matter who or what was pushing the pointer, Tibby knew the Ouija board was right. Veronica needed help. And so did Tibby. The clock was still ticking away their minutes together.

Please let me stay with Veronica. Praise His holy name and let me stay. Praise . . . stay . . . praise . . . stay.

Tibby waited for a miracle. Maybe a telephone call telling Veronica she didn't have to go to Fort Wayne in the morning. Or maybe a way for Tibby to go with her.

But the telephone didn't ring and a miracle didn't happen.

Tibby slipped out of her bed and tiptoed over to Veronica's. She stood at the edge of her bed, very still, and waited for Veronica to wake up. She remembered that standing like that, just standing, used to be enough to awaken Mrs. Wilson. "What's wrong, baby?" Mrs. Wilson would say. "Have you had a bad dream? C'mon, get in bed with me." Then Tibby would climb into her warm bed and Mrs. Wilson would hug her and murmur, "It's okay, it's okay," until Tibby finally fell asleep.

But Veronica didn't wake up.

Tibby touched her shoulder, lightly.

Veronica jumped. "Wha — who's there?"

"It's me. Tibby."

Veronica looked at the clock. "It's almost three o'clock in the morning. What do you want?"

"I want to go with you tomorrow."

"Well, you can't. Now go to sleep."

"But I don't want to go back to Aunt Evelyn. I want to stay with *you*."

"God, Tib. Let me get some sleep."

"Sure." Tibby backed away. She was too big to get into bed with her mother anyway. And Veronica needed her sleep.

Tibby went back to her own bed and lay there, with her eyes wide open.

Please let me stay with Veronica. Praise His holy name and let me stay. Praise . . . stay . . . praise . . . stay.

But she had the feeling no one was listening.

CHAPTER 11

I T WAS raining when Tibby's plane landed, and Aunt Evelyn was wearing a clear plastic rain bonnet, the kind that snapped under her chin, even though it was perfectly dry inside the airport.

"How was your trip?" she asked, brushing Tibby's cheek with a kiss.

"Okay."

"And how is Veronica?"

"Okay."

"Did she say when she's coming home?"

"No."

Aunt Evelyn kept up her questions down the concourse, around the luggage area, and in the car. What did Tibby do while Veronica was working all day? Where did they stay? Did Tibby meet anyone famous?

After she asked every question she could think

of, Aunt Evelyn told Tibby what had gone on while she was away. She'd gone back to her own house, and she'd found aphids attacking her young chrysanthemum plants. She'd had to call a plumber to check a leak from her water heater. And she wasn't sure, but she thought there might be a mouse in her garage.

Lord, what excitement.

Finally the old woman shut up, but only because she had to concentrate on the problem of finding her car and getting it out of the airport parking lot. She took the wrong ramp twice before she stopped to ask an attendant how to get back on the road to Seneca. His directions confused her more, and they circled the short-term parking area two more times before she stopped and asked another attendant for advice. He drew a little map on the back of a parking ticket, and Aunt Evelyn followed it to get out of the parking lot and onto the Illinois Toll Road.

And to think Veronica knew every building on the Washington Mall.

"I was a little surprised when Veronica called," Aunt Evelyn said, once they were safely on the toll road. "I was hoping you'd be able to stay through the weekend."

"Don't worry," Tibby said. "I didn't want to come back."

"No," Aunt Evelyn said, without taking her eyes off the road. "I'm sure you didn't."

"And I can take care of myself, so you don't have to worry about changing any plans."

"That's not what I meant."

Tibby didn't care what she meant. She just stared at the rainy road ahead. The road that was taking her farther and farther from the airport. Farther and farther from Veronica.

The rain had slowed to a drizzle by the time they pulled into their driveway. Inside the house, Lou Grant danced in his jerky way around Aunt Evelyn's feet.

"Look who's home, Louie," she crooned. "Tibby!"

But Lou Grant didn't care about Tibby. And Tibby didn't care about him, either. She took her suitcase and Thai kite upstairs and set them just inside her door. Then, without changing clothes, she headed for Solimano's lot.

She didn't see Verl on the manicured grass or near the circular garden. She went up the slope to the Indian campground.

"Verl!" she called. "Verl!"

He didn't answer, and Tibby didn't know what she'd say if he did. Maybe, "Hey, Verl, what's up? I praised His crummy name, but I had to come home anyway. How come?" Esther was probably still waiting for her Barbie doll, too. The poor kid. Somebody should tell her.

At the top of the slope she looked and called again. But no one answered. She started down the path to the river. It was wet, and her shoes sank into the mud.

"Hey, there!" a voice called behind her.

Tibby turned. It was old Solimano, at the top of the hill.

"What are you doing there?" he called, starting down toward her. "Oh, it's you, Verl's friend. What are you doing back here?"

"I'm looking for Verl."

"He's not here. Ground's too wet to work." He looked at Tibby as if she should have known that.

"I thought maybe he came anyway, just to mess around."

Mr. Solimano shook his head. "I'd know if he did. He always checks with me before he comes back here." His tone of voice said that's what Tibby should have done, too.

"Yeah, well." Tibby headed back up the hill, toward the street.

"Why don't you see if he's home?"

"I don't know where he lives."

"You don't? Aren't you one of them?" He looked at her. "No, I guess not. Do you know where they go to church?"

Tibby nodded.

"His family lives in an old trailer behind the barn. And how they get all those kids in that one little trailer, I'll never know." He chuckled. "I guess it just shows what a little faith can do."

Tibby headed back down the river road and turned when she came to the muddy tire tracks that led to the bright yellow barn. She still didn't know what she'd say to Verl — or whether she'd say anything at all — but at least she'd see where he lived.

As she got close to the barn, she saw hand-painted red letters above its door:

ASSEMBLY OF BELIEVERS
in the
LORD GOD ALMIGHTY

The door was shut, but Tibby heard hammering and boards being moved inside, so she went wide around the barn until she saw an old blue trailer on the other side. A narrow gully separated the barn from the trailer, and water was running through the gully. A mess of kids took turns jumping across it. Esther was one of them, wearing that dress with empty belt loops again.

"What are you doing here?"

Tibby spun around. It was Verl, in overalls sprinkled with sawdust.

"You scared me," she said.

"What are you doing here?" he asked again.

"Oh . . . I . . . uh."

He looked at her. "Something's wrong."

"Not really."

"Yes, there is."

Tibby felt a knot loosening in her throat. "It's just that I prayed and prayed," she said, "but I still had to come home."

"Without your mother."

Tibby nodded. She was afraid she'd cry if she spoke again.

Esther came running toward them. "What's wrong?" she asked.

"Tibby had to come home without her mother," Verl told her.

Esther nodded. "I thought she got what she wanted too fast," she said. "She's got to pray more."

"Yeah," Verl said. "Maybe so."

Tibby turned on him. "But I did pray. All night long." Nobody could pray harder than Tibby had in the hotel room last night.

Verl looked at her, helpless.

But Esther knew the answer. "You've got to get other people to pray with you," she said. "The Lord listens better if there's lots of people praying. Isn't that right, Verl?"

"Yeah," Verl said, with his eyes still on Tibby. "I guess so."

But what other people would pray for Tibby?

"You should come to meeting," Esther said. "You should come tonight, so's people can start praying right away."

"Meeting?" Tibby asked, and Verl nodded toward the barn. She looked again at the sign over the barn door:

ASSEMBLY OF BELIEVERS
in the
LORD GOD ALMIGHTY

And she remembered what the Ouija board had said: B-E-L-I-E-V-E.

"Will you come, Tibby?" Esther asked. "Will you?"

"Maybe she doesn't want to," Verl said. "And she probably shouldn't, because her aunt . . ."

His voice trailed off, and Tibby guessed he was remembering the way Aunt Evelyn had slammed the door in his father's face.

"I want to come," Tibby said. "I really do."

CHAPTER 12

TIBBY told Aunt Evelyn she was going for a bike ride after dinner.

"By yourself?"

Tibby nodded.

"Well, stay on this street, and be sure to come in when it starts to get dark."

"Okay." Tibby smiled sweetly and took off for the bright yellow barn.

The barn was painted bright yellow on the inside, too. Tibby looked for a pulpit or some kind of altar, but there wasn't any. Just rows and rows of benches arranged around an empty space where a microphone hung from the rafters.

She followed Verl to a front-row seat near the hanging microphone. Esther was already there, and so were three younger kids and a red-haired woman with a baby.

"Mama, this is Tibby," Verl said to the red-haired woman.

Mrs. Milner didn't wear any makeup or fingernail polish, and her faded gray dress hung loose on her. She had clear blue eyes, though, and she became almost pretty when she smiled and reached out to squeeze Tibby's hand. "I'm so glad the Lord brought you here, Tibby," she said.

She scooted over and patted the seat next to her, indicating that Tibby should sit down. Tibby would have preferred to sit in the back of the barn, by herself, but she didn't see that she had a choice. She sat down, and Verl sat next to her.

The barn was filling with people, mainly families with small children. The girls and women all wore dresses, and Tibby began to feel uncomfortable in her jeans. Nobody else seemed to notice, though. They all smiled — warm, friendly smiles, like Veronica's.

Just across from Tibby, on the other side of the microphone, two men were tuning their guitars and a woman was testing her flute. Verl's father was there, too, tapping a tambourine softly against his thigh as he looked over the crowd.

Suddenly one of the guitarists shouted, "I feel the Lord!" And he started strumming.

"Amen, brother!" cried the flutist, and she put her instrument to her lips.

"Praise the Lord!" shouted Verl's father, as he

joined in. Then all the people in the barn were on their feet, clapping or waving their arms, and singing,

> *Let us sing together!*
> *Let us pray together!*
> *Let us praise the Lord God above!*
> *For his wonders are never ceasing*
> *And his love always increasing.*
> *So let us sing together!*
> *Let us pray together!*
> *Let us praise the Lord God above!*

The people on the other side of the Milner family broke into a dance that carried them into the open space around the microphone. Verl's mother took hold of Tibby's hand, and Tibby was afraid she'd get dragged into a dance, too. She dug her heels into the dirt floor and looked around for the nearest exit. But Mrs. Milner didn't start dancing — she just swayed to the music — and Tibby stayed.

When the song ended, everyone shouted "Amen!" "Hallelujah!" and "Praise His holy name!" Then they settled back on their benches, and the guitarist who had started it all stepped up to the microphone and asked, "Has anyone been touched by the Lord today?"

"Oh, yes! Oh, yes!" several shouted.

The guitarist pointed to a man in the back. "Tell us about it, brother!" Everyone turned to watch the man — a skinny, bald guy — hurry to the microphone.

He blew into the microphone a couple of times

and then began: "Last night I told you I was in the depths of financial despair, and we prayed together."

"Oh, yes, we prayed!" a woman cried.

"And I became filled with the knowledge that bounty comes from faithfulness."

"Yes, it does! Yes, it does!" another woman agreed.

"Then I went home last night and turned to my Bible for comfort and guidance," he said. "And when I opened the good book, what do you think I found?"

"What did you find? Tell us, brother!"

"A five-hundred-dollar bill!" He pulled the bill from his pocket and held it up for everyone to see.

A general gasp ran through the barn, then: "Praise the Lord!" "Hallelujah!" "The Lord takes care of His chosen ones!" Tibby was impressed. She never knew God ran around sticking money in Bibles.

The man raised his hands in praise and walked, trembling, back to his seat. Then a woman stepped up to the microphone and told about a lump in her breast that had miraculously disappeared. And another woman, with a baby, told how the child had been born dead but started breathing when they prayed over him. A man stood up and shouted some strange syllables, and everyone praised the Lord for that.

Tibby wanted to hear about more miracles, but

Verl's father went to the microphone next. "We have a new child of God with us tonight," he said. "A child that was brought to us by my own children." He held out his hand to Tibby, and she felt her heart take a running leap at her throat. "Come here, child," he said.

Tibby sat frozen, but Mrs. Milner gently nudged her out of her seat. "Go on, honey," she said. "The Lord loves you and will take care of you."

Tibby looked at Verl, who shrugged, as if to say it was up to her. On the other side of him, Esther grinned. "Go on, Tibby," she whispered. "Go on. For your mama."

Tibby stood up and took Mr. Milner's outstretched hand.

"This child needs our prayers," he told the Believers, "because her mother has a job — "

"A mother working," a voice moaned.

" — that takes her away from her home and family for weeks at a time."

"No, Lord, no."

"So let us pray together for this child and her mother. Let us pray that her mother will come home to her rightful place beside this child — and will join our circle of Believers in the Lord God Almighty."

Tibby looked at the rows of smiling, nodding faces. They were so sure that anything they prayed for would happen. And why shouldn't they be sure? Didn't that guy find five hundred dollars in his Bible right after the meeting last night? And if God could come up with five hundred dollars, couldn't He bring a kid's mother home?

Then the music started up again, and Tibby walked back to her seat. Mrs. Milner squeezed her hand while everyone sang,

> *Amazing grace, how sweet thou art*
> *That saved a wretch like me!*
> *I once was lost but now am found,*
> *Was blind but now I see.*
>
> *'Twas grace that taught my heart to fear,*
> *And grace my fears relieved;*
> *How precious did that grace appear*
> *The hour I first believed!*

They continued singing, about toils and snares and bright shining suns. When they finished, a door behind the musicians opened, and a heavyset man in a white suit strode to the microphone.

"Brother Ralph!" a voice cried. "Bless us!"

The white-suited man turned toward the voice. "I'm not the one who blesses you, brother," he said. "It's the Lord God Almighty who blesses us all!"

"Amen!" several shouted. "Hallelujah!"

They probably would have kept on shouting praise, but Brother Ralph grabbed the microphone and drowned them out. "Brothers and sisters!" he cried. "I'm gonna blacken the eye of the devil tonight!"

The people went crazy, clapping and shouting and raising their hands in praise. Brother Ralph nodded and smiled, then held the microphone so close that Tibby thought he was going to eat it.

"Now the devil is a sneaky fellow," he said, with his eyes narrowed and his voice real low. "He's always tryin' to raise a false god in front of us. The false god of *med*-i-cine, the false god of life in-*sur*-ance, the false god of ed-u-*ca*-tion, the false god of *seat* belts in our cars. The devil wants us to think these gods can protect us from the dangers and evils of the world. But can they? I ask you, brothers and sisters, can they?"

"No!" everyone shouted. Brother Ralph stepped back from the microphone and beamed at them all.

"Of course not," he said. "These false gods can't protect us from a thing. Only the Lord God Almighty can protect and save us!"

Then Brother Ralph told how the Lord God Almighty had helped people. How he'd ended one woman's twenty years of pain from arthritis, and how he'd moved a man's stalled car from the railroad tracks. He spoke in a rhythmic way that had people swaying in their seats.

Many people shouted praise and thanksgiving, but Tibby just gasped at each new miracle. Why had she never heard of all this before? A God that could move cars off railroad tracks! Surely he could bring Veronica home.

Then the music started again, and Brother Ralph called on all Believers to come receive the Lord. Tibby hesitated for just a moment. Then she lined up with Verl and his mother and everyone else.

When Brother Ralph laid his hands on her head, she knew, *just knew*, Veronica was coming home.

Verl joined some other boys in passing baskets around the barn, and people dropped money into them. Tibby wished she still had the money Veronica had given her in Washington. She would have given it all — all fifty dollars — to Brother Ralph and the Lord.

CHAPTER 13

I T WAS dark by the time Tibby got home.

"Where have you been?" Aunt Evelyn wasn't any louder than the voices in the barn, but she was so much shriller, so much less blessed. "I called the police, and . . . oh, dear."

A patrol car pulled up in front of the house, and Tibby went upstairs to her room while Aunt Evelyn went out to meet the officers. When she came back inside, she wasn't as shrill, but she still wanted to know where Tibby had been.

"With a friend."

"Not that boy who came to the door with his father."

"What if it was?"

"Did he talk to you about God?"

"What if he did?"

"Those people are dangerous, Tibby. There was

a story in the paper about them while you were away. A young woman died in childbirth because they wouldn't call a doctor. They prayed over her instead."

"You've got it all wrong," Tibby said. "That woman didn't die. I saw her tonight. And they *saved* her baby by praying over it."

Aunt Evelyn looked at her. "I don't know what they've told you, Tibby, but I want you to stay away from them. Do you understand?"

Tibby nodded. She understood, all right.

The next day was Sunday, and Aunt Evelyn asked Tibby if she'd like to go to church with her.

"Church?"

"I thought you might want to come," Aunt Evelyn said, "now that you're so interested in religion."

Tibby almost laughed. She wasn't interested in religion. She was interested in miracles.

Later, on the path by the river, Tibby told Verl what Aunt Evelyn had said about staying away from the Believers.

"You'd better not come again," he said. " 'Honor thy father and thy mother.' "

"She's not my father *or* my mother," Tibby said. "She's just my mother's crazy old aunt."

"But you shouldn't make her worry so."

"You don't know Aunt Evelyn," Tibby said. "She worries about *everything*. She'd worry if I stayed home."

Verl still didn't look convinced.

"Okay," Tibby said, "I'll make sure she doesn't worry."

"Don't lie," he warned.

"I won't lie," Tibby said. Not much.

That afternoon she asked Aunt Evelyn if they could eat dinner early, around five-thirty.

"But we'd miss the news," Aunt Evelyn said. "And you know Veronica always gets more air time on weekends."

"I know," Tibby said, with genuine sadness. "But maybe we could tape it. I have to work on a social studies project at a friend's house."

Aunt Evelyn eyed her suspiciously. "What friend?"

Patsy Franklin would be too easy to check, so Tibby picked a name from her class: "Katie Carlson."

"Katie Carlson? Why haven't I ever heard you mention her before?"

"I don't know her very well. Mrs. Crawley just assigned us to work together." Tibby smiled sweetly. "We're studying Bolivia."

"Where does she live?"

"Just around the corner. On Riverview Drive."

"I'll give you a ride," Aunt Evelyn said, "so you won't be out alone after dark."

"Oh, don't bother." Tibby kept smiling. "I'll head home early."

"Well, if it gets dark, give me a call. I don't want

to have to call the police again." Aunt Evelyn laughed, a little nervously.

"Don't worry. I'll be back."

Aunt Evelyn looked at her carefully. "I'm going to trust you on this, Tibby. But if you're not back . . ."

"Don't worry!"

Tibby went upstairs and rummaged through her closet, trying to find something dowdy that would make her look like the other Believers. But her closet was full of Veronica's red. The only thing she could come up with was the navy-blue skirt that went with her St. Agnes uniform. She knew she couldn't leave the house in that without arousing Aunt Evelyn's suspicions again, so she stuffed it in her schoolbag. She'd have to change clothes on the path by the river.

That night Brother Ralph warned the Believers that sometimes they had to be patient with God.

"The Lord likes to test us," he said, "to see if we truly believe. He tested Abraham. He tested Job. And sometimes, when we're praying for something very important, He tests us. We may have to wait and pray a long, long time. We may think the Lord doesn't hear us. But He does. He's just testing us to see if we *really* believe in Him. And if we pass the Lord's test, He'll answer our every prayer."

So Tibby knew she'd have to be patient.

She left the meeting early, before Brother

Ralph's final blessing, so she could get home before dark. But she managed to go back the next night, and the night after that, too. Each time she heard of more miracles, and each time the Believers prayed with her for Veronica's return.

CHAPTER 14

TIBBY always sat with the Milners at meetings, and Mrs. Milner asked her if she'd like to come to their trailer for supper on Tuesday. "Then we could all come to meeting together," Mrs. Milner said.

So Tibby told Aunt Evelyn that Katie's mother had invited her to dinner.

"I don't know," Aunt Evelyn said. "You've spent so much time there already. Why don't you invite Katie over here instead?"

Tibby had an answer ready. "We're using some *National Geographics* at her house," she said, "and Katie's father doesn't want us to take them anywhere."

Aunt Evelyn nodded. "*The National Geographic* is a wonderful magazine," she said. "Veronica's mother — your grandmother — used to subscribe.

Maybe I still have some over at my house. If I do, you and Katie could — "

"Don't worry," Tibby said. "Katie's father has a complete set — from about 1900, I think."

"My goodness," Aunt Evelyn said. "Well, the least I can do is make a cheesecake or something, as a sort of thank-you gift."

"Okay." The Milners would like a cheesecake.

As Tibby went around the yellow barn the next day, she saw four kids outside, taking turns leaping across the gully.

"There she is!" one of the little ones cried. "There's Tibby! And she's got something!"

They all came running to her, and Verl came around from the back of the trailer.

"You've seen everybody before," he said, "but I don't guess you know their names."

"She knows mine!" Esther cried. "Don't you, Tibby?"

"I sure do." Tibby grinned, and Esther strutted a little in front of the others.

"Tibby's known *me* for a long time."

"Well, this here's Naomi." Verl pointed to one a little smaller than Esther. "And here's Jeremiah and Ezekiel. The baby, Ruth, is inside with Mama."

The children kept their eyes on the package in Tibby's hand.

"It's cheesecake," she said. "For dessert."

"A *cheese* cake?" Esther looked disappointed, and Tibby laughed. She remembered how she used to think a cheesecake must be a hunk of Velveeta with cottage cheese piled on top.

"Don't worry," Tibby said. "It's like a pie, and it tastes good."

"Is it sweet?" Esther asked.

Tibby nodded, and everyone looked at the package hungrily.

"C'mon," Verl said. "Let's take it in to Mama."

Verl carried the cheesecake, Naomi and Esther took Tibby by the hand, and the little boys followed close behind. It was dark inside the trailer, and it took a moment for Tibby's eyes to adjust to the light. Then she saw Verl's mother standing in a kitchen about the size of Veronica's walk-in closet. With Ruth resting on one hip, Mrs. Milner stood at the stove and stirred a pot with a broken handle.

"Mama! Mama!" Naomi cried. "Tibby brought us something!"

"It's sweet, and it's to eat!" Esther grinned at her own cleverness. "Hey, that rhymes!"

"It's cheesecake," Tibby said. "My aunt sent it."

"Isn't that nice!" Mrs. Milner took the package from Verl and smiled at Tibby. "But I hate to think of your aunt going to all that trouble, just for us."

"It wasn't any trouble," Tibby said. "She wanted to do it."

"You'll have to thank her for us, honey." Mrs. Milner looked down at the pot she was stirring. "I hope you like bott pies," she said. "They're not fancy, but . . ."

"I love them." Tibby had no idea what bott pies

were, but they smelled good, and she liked being called honey.

"Can I sit next to Tibby at supper?" Esther asked. "I've known her the longest."

"*Verl* met her first," Naomi reminded her sister. "And he says *I* can sit next to her at supper."

Verl looked surprised.

"Hush up," their mother said. "You're going to frighten Tibby away."

The little girls both grinned at Tibby.

"Now, all of you," Mrs. Milner said, "get out of here so I have room to turn around."

"Oh, Mama . . ."

"I mean it. I can't get supper on the table if you're all hanging on me."

Tibby turned to go with the others.

"Except Tibby," Mrs. Milner said. "I'd like Tibby to stay and give me a hand." She looked at Tibby. "If that's all right."

Tibby nodded, and the others moved back outside, grumbling about their positions at the supper table. Tibby looked around the tiny kitchen and wondered where this table was. The only other room in view was small, too, and it was already cramped with two old couches and a stack of brown cardboard boxes, all marked "Glory Bound Publishing Co., Inc."

"Would you mind stirring, Tibby, while I cut the greens?" Mrs. Milner asked.

Tibby moved over to her place by the stove and dipped the wooden spoon into a yellow broth bubbling with squares of dough, tiny bits of chicken, carrots, and celery tops. So this was bott pies.

"My, it's nice to have a girl in the kitchen again," Mrs. Milner said. "Verl tries, and so does Esther sometimes, but it's not the same. They just don't know what to do, the way Dawn did. But I guess Verl's told you about Dawn."

Tibby shook her head.

"Really? I'm surprised. They were so close." Mrs. Milner stopped cutting for a moment. Then she spoke softly, but matter-of-factly. "Dawn was our second oldest, just a year behind Verl. She died, a year ago Christmas."

Tibby didn't know what to say.

"I know she's happy with the Lord, but still I miss her." Mrs. Milner cleared her throat and smiled at Tibby. "Especially when there's a meal to get on the table."

Tibby tried to stir the bott pies carefully, the way Dawn would have.

Ruth started fussing.

"It never fails," Mrs. Milner said. "Just when I'm ready to serve things up, the baby starts. Here, would you take her a minute?"

Ruth wailed louder when Mrs. Milner plopped her into Tibby's arms. The baby was heavier than she looked, and Tibby staggered a bit.

"Can you handle her?" Mrs. Milner asked.

"Sure," Tibby lied. "We're fine." She carried the baby out to the room with the couches.

This was the first time Tibby had ever held a baby, and she tried to hold her gently, the way she thought babies were supposed to be held. But Ruth wasn't a gentle baby. She kept hollering and splatting her wet hands against Tibby's face. Tibby tightened her grip on the kid so she wouldn't drop her. She bet Dawn never dropped a baby.

She expected Ruth to wail even louder, under that tightened grip. But the baby stopped, except for a few little sucking noises. Evidently the kid liked being held like that.

Then Tibby felt Ruth jerk a little, and she heard a low, froglike noise. She smelled something funny, and she looked at her shoulder. Her blouse was soaking up some milky stuff, with little white lumps in it.

"Oh Lor — " Tibby caught herself. The Milners only spoke of the Lord in praise. She was sure they didn't mention Him when a kid spit up.

"Is everything all right?" Mrs. Milner called from the kitchen.

"Everything's fine," Tibby said, looking around for a napkin or handkerchief. She didn't see any, so she pulled up the bottom edge of Ruth's cotton shirt and dabbed at her shoulder.

"Supper's ready," Mrs. Milner announced. She went to the front door and called, "Jeremiah! Ezekiel! Go get your father!"

Without being called, the other kids hurried into the kitchen. Verl picked up the pot of bott pies, Esther picked up the bowl of greens, and Naomi took a stack of plates. Then they headed out the door again.

Mrs. Milner brought the cheesecake, and Tibby, still carrying Ruth, followed them.

They trooped around to the back of the trailer, where there was a crude picnic table, with no benches. Tibby guessed they were going to eat standing up.

But then she saw Mr. Milner carrying two wooden benches from the meeting barn.

"Papa! Papa!" Naomi called. "Tibby's going to eat with us tonight!"

"Praise the Lord!" he said.

"And she brought us a dessert!" Esther said.

"Well, let's praise the Lord even more!" He winked at Tibby, then set the benches down, saying, "Here's the rest of the dining room furniture."

"Thank you, Paul," Mrs. Milner said as she adjusted the benches around the table.

"Thank *the Lord*," he said, correcting her.

Mrs. Milner smiled and nodded. "Thank the Lord."

CHAPTER 15

"LORD God Almighty," Mr. Milner said, and all heads went down as everyone — even Ruth — joined hands around the picnic table. "We thank You for bringing us here together again, and we especially thank You for bringing our sister Tibby to share this food with us. We ask You to bless us and bless the food we eat. And we ask You to remember our brothers and sisters who are suffering tonight."

He went on and named some brothers and sisters whose sufferings were especially bad. Tibby didn't hear that, though. She just kept hearing the words *our sister Tibby*. They sounded good.

Finally the suffering ended, and everyone said, "Amen."

"So," Mr. Milner said as he dished out the bott pies, "who wants to play the Bible game?"

Hands shot up all around the table.

Mr. Milner laughed. "Put your hands down." He nodded to Ezekiel first. "Who led the Israelites out of Egypt?"

"MO-ses," Ezekiel said, in a loud, clear voice.

"Bless you, child!" Mr. Milner said, and Ezekiel beamed. "Now, Jeremiah, it's your turn. What did the Lord do so Moses and the Israelites could get away from the Egyptians?"

"He parted the Red Sea." Jeremiah pronounced the words carefully.

"Bless you, child!" Mr. Milner kept dishing out the bott pies. "Naomi, do you know what Moses destroyed?"

"The golden calf," she said.

"Bless you, child!" Mr. Milner said, and Naomi grinned at Tibby.

"It's my turn," Esther said. "Don't forget me."

Mr. Milner laughed. "How could I ever forget you? You can tell us why Moses destroyed the golden calf."

"Because the Israelites were honoring it when they should have been honoring the Lord God above."

"Bless you, child!" Mr. Milner said. "You know your Bible well!"

Esther looked around the table, triumphant.

Mr. Milner handed out the last plate, and the children all turned to watch their mother take the first bite before they began eating. After Mr. Milner tasted the bott pies, he smacked his lips.

"Oh, Judith," he said, "I can tell the Lord was with you in the kitchen!"

Mrs. Milner blushed.

"Now I have to think up a good one for Verl," Mr. Milner said.

"No, no," Esther said. "Tibby's the next oldest."

"Maybe Tibby doesn't want to play," Mrs. Milner suggested.

"I'll play," Tibby said. Mrs. Wilson used to tell her Bible stories, so she knew all about Moses.

"All right, Tibby," Mr. Milner said, smiling at her. "What was the name of the first man God created?"

Tibby looked down at her plate. He'd given her a question so simple that Ruth could have answered it.

"It begins with the letter *A*," Esther hinted.

Tibby looked at Mr. Milner. "Could you give me another question? Please?"

"Well . . ." Mr. Milner hesitated.

"I want to answer one like the others."

Verl grinned across the table at her, and Mr. Milner smiled. "All right, Tibby," he said. "I'll treat you like a Milner. How did God first appear to Moses?"

"In a burning bush," she said, grinning back at Verl.

"Bless you, child!" Mr. Milner said, just as if she were one of his own.

Tibby thought Verl would get a question about Moses, too, but Mr. Milner had something else for him.

"Verl, do you recognize this?" he asked. " 'A wise

man maketh a glad father: but a foolish son is the heaviness of his mother.' "

Verl joined in: " 'Treasures of wickedness profit nothing: but righteousness delivereth from death.' "

"You recognize it," Mr. Milner said.

Verl nodded. "Proverbs ten, verses one and two."

"Bless you, son."

After supper Verl and his father carried the benches back to the barn, and Tibby helped Mrs. Milner and the little girls clear the table. She knew what Veronica would say about that, with the females getting stuck with the dishes.

Ruth fussed the whole time they were cleaning up. When they finished, Mrs. Milner went into the little room with the couches in it and sat down.

"What have you heard from your mother?" Mrs. Milner asked as she unbuttoned her blouse. Tibby tried not to watch, but Mrs. Milner was uncovering one of her breasts and offering its bright pink nipple to Ruth. The baby grabbed it hungrily and started sucking.

Naomi and Esther played on the floor, as if a bare boob was the most natural thing in the world.

"What have you heard from her?" Mrs. Milner asked again.

"Who?" Tibby pried her eyes off Mrs. Milner's breast.

"Your mother," Mrs. Milner said patiently. "Have you heard from her?"

"Oh, my mother." Tibby gulped and looked

around the room, at anything but Mrs. Milner and that bare boob. "I don't know. She should be coming home soon."

Esther climbed up on the couch, next to her mother. "Why's it taking so long?"

"I don't know, honey," her mother said. "It's not for us to understand the ways of the Lord."

"He's taking a long time with my Barbie doll, too," Esther said.

"I know, honey." Mrs. Milner rumpled Esther's hair. "Tell us about your mother, Tibby. What's she like?"

Naomi and Esther looked interested, too.

Tibby didn't know what to say. How could she describe Veronica? The way she laughed, the way she smiled, the way people looked at her.

"Well," Tibby began, "she's very pretty."

Esther nodded. "I knew it."

"Esther," Mrs. Milner said, "we don't care how a person looks on the outside. The important thing is how that person looks on the inside, in the eyes of the Lord."

"Oh, the Lord thinks she's pretty, too," Tibby said quickly, and Mrs. Milner smiled.

"Then why," asked Mr. Milner from the doorway behind Tibby, "isn't she home with you?"

Tibby was surprised he'd been listening. "She has to work," she said.

"Putting her job before her family," Mr. Milner said, "does not make her pretty in the eyes of the Lord."

101

Tibby turned and looked at him. What did he mean?

"I'm sure Tibby's mother loves her very much," Mrs. Milner said gently.

"Yes, I'm sure she does," Mr. Milner said, "but we need to pray for her. Are you ready to go to meeting?"

Mrs. Milner looked down at Ruth, still sucking. "We'll be ready in just a minute."

Tibby carried Ruth over to the barn and followed Mrs. Milner to their front-row seats. Several people smiled and nodded. Not the way they did the first night, to welcome a stranger. This time they smiled and nodded like they knew she belonged. She wondered if maybe she reminded them, just a little, of Dawn.

CHAPTER 16

VERL had told Tibby that he would be working at Solimano's lot the next day, so she went there right after school. Verl wasn't there, but he arrived about ten minutes later.

"Where have you been?" Tibby asked.

"I just work after school," Verl said.

"But you don't go to school."

"Mr. Solimano doesn't know that." Verl grinned, and Tibby grinned back. It was nice to know that Verl — good, honest Verl — knew how to bend the rules a little.

Tibby offered to help Verl with his weeding and planting, but he shook his head.

"Mr. Solimano wants this done just so," he said. "I'd better do it myself."

Tibby sat down to watch him, but she soon got bored and decided to climb the hill to the old

Indian campground. She followed its path and tried to imagine the people who lived there hundreds of years ago. She could almost see an old man climbing the hill to the lookout. Or a toddler chasing butterflies.

Finally she went over to the rock box and pulled out the old checkered shirt that held the prayer stick. She unwrapped the stick and ran her fingers across its small indentations. She wondered who had held this stick before and what they had prayed for.

Maybe a young brave had held it before his first hunt. Or maybe a mother as she prayed for her sick baby. Or maybe, just maybe, a girl had held it while she waited for her mother to come home.

Lord, please send Veronica home. Praise Your holy name and send Veronica home. Praise . . . Veronica . . . praise . . . Veronica.

Tibby hurried home that afternoon, ready to tell Aunt Evelyn that she was late because of a trip she and Katie had made to the library. But when she came in, she didn't need an excuse. Aunt Evelyn was on the phone in the kitchen, with her back to the door.

"Ann Arbor!" she said. "But I thought you were coming home after Fort Wayne!" So Tibby knew something else had come up. She stood in the doorway, listening.

"But I'm not her mother," Aunt Evelyn said.

"This is your responsibility, not mine. And she — "

Tibby didn't want to hear the rest. She closed the door quietly and went upstairs to her room, to get ready for meeting. The Lord was expecting an awful lot of patience.

Tibby went to the blue trailer before meeting so there would be time to sit and talk with Mrs. Milner while she nursed Ruth. She went early the next night, too. Mrs. Milner's bare breast didn't bother her at all anymore.

The Milners had had cabbage for dinner that night, and Mrs. Milner said the trailer still smelled from the cooking. So they went out back to the picnic table, and Verl came over to join them.

Tibby noticed that the bare breast didn't bother him, either.

"Have you heard anything from your mother?" Mrs. Milner asked.

"She's in Ann Arbor," Tibby said, "covering another story."

"What will you do if she never comes home?" Verl asked.

"Verl." Mrs. Milner reached across the picnic table and took Tibby's hand. "What kind of question is that? Of course her mother will come."

"But what if she comes and doesn't stay?" Verl asked. "What if she just leaves right away, on another story?"

"That's why we're praying," Mrs. Milner said.

"But sometimes," he said carefully, "the Lord doesn't answer prayers exactly the way we want. You know that, Mama."

Mrs. Milner squeezed Tibby's hand so hard that it hurt. "This is different, Verl."

How was it different? From what? But something in their voices kept Tibby from asking.

Everyone praised and prayed especially hard that night. It was as if they all had the feeling that a miracle was going to take place.

"I feel the Lord is working His wonders among us," Brother Ralph said. "Can you feel it, brothers and sisters? Can you?"

"Oh, yes!" they shouted. "We feel it!"

Tibby felt it. Verl was smiling at her, so she knew he must feel it, too. Veronica was probably on the plane at this very moment.

So she wasn't surprised, when she got home, to hear that Veronica had called.

"She has something to tell you," Aunt Evelyn said, "and I told her you'd call back."

Tibby's fingers trembled as she dialed the number Aunt Evelyn gave her. She wished the Milners and Brother Ralph and all the Believers could be with her, to witness the miracle.

The phone rang at the other end, and Tibby kept breathing, *Thank You, Lord, thank You.*

Veronica answered. "Oh, hi, Tib," she said. "How's your project coming along?"

"What project?"

"Bolivia." Veronica laughed. "How could you forget? Aunt E says you've been working on it night and day."

"Oh, *that* project. It's . . . uh . . . fine." *But tell me about the miracle.*

Veronica laughed again, this time nervously. "I don't know *why* Aunt E couldn't give you this message, but she wanted me to tell you myself."

Tibby waited.

"There's a financial crisis in Columbus."

Tibby didn't understand.

"Thousands of people could lose their life savings. They're camping out in front of the savings-and-loan associations, trying to get in."

Tibby still didn't understand.

"This is a big story, Tib. It may take several weeks."

So. There was no miracle. Just Veronica going off on another story.

"But you haven't been home for so long," Tibby almost whispered.

"I know, Tib. But we had that time in Washington."

"It was so short. Can't somebody else cover it?"

"This is a big story, Tib."

"Can't I come with you? I could help."

"You've got school," Veronica said, "and, besides, I work better when I don't have to worry about other people."

But I'm not other people, Tibby wanted to say. I'm your daughter.

But she didn't say anything.

When Tibby hung up, she saw Aunt Evelyn standing in the doorway, watching her. "Maybe this is for the best," the old woman finally said. "You and I — both of us — have to stop waiting for Veronica to come home."

"She'll come," Tibby insisted.

But when?

Tibby lay awake almost all night.

Why, Lord, why?

When she'd been praying so hard and when she felt the miracle coming, why did He hurt her like that? Didn't the Lord love her? Didn't He care?

Didn't He exist?

For a few minutes, just a few, Tibby almost stopped believing. Then she remembered what Brother Ralph had said. The Lord tested Abraham. The Lord tested Job.

And now He was testing Tibby.

CHAPTER 17

TIBBY went directly to the blue trailer after school the next day. Mrs. Milner was outside, hanging wash on a line that had been strung from the trailer to a tree.

"Why, Tibby," she said, "what are you doing here?"

"My mother's not coming home," Tibby said softly. "For a long time."

The words seemed to echo around her.

"Oh, honey." Mrs. Milner dropped one of her husband's clean, wet undershirts in the grass. She put her arms around Tibby and held her close.

"Sometimes life can be so hard," Mrs. Milner said. "But we'll just have to pray harder, won't we?"

Tibby nodded and felt her cheek rub against Mrs. Milner's soft breast.

"Maybe," she said timidly, "maybe I could live with you. Until my mother comes home."

Mrs. Milner squeezed her. "I would love that, Tibby. We all would. But we couldn't take you away from your aunt."

Tibby thought Aunt Evelyn would be relieved to get rid of her — of the *responsibility* — but she didn't argue. If the Milners didn't have room for a table they could all eat around, they sure didn't have room for another kid.

Tibby stayed at the blue trailer for about an hour. She helped Mrs. Milner hang out the rest of the wash — even Verl's underwear — and she took Ruth for a walk in the rickety stroller. She left around four o'clock, so she would have time to finish her homework before meeting.

When she got home, though, Aunt Evelyn had other plans. She'd brought Tibby's dragon kite down from her room, and she wanted to fly it.

"Fly it?" Tibby hadn't touched the kite since she'd brought it home, still in its package, from Washington.

"Why not?" Aunt Evelyn said. "It's a beautiful day, with just enough wind for flying a kite."

"But . . ." Tibby wondered what had happened to the precious schedule.

"The problem is, there are so many wires and trees around here. But I know a farmer, just past the edge of town, who always used to let us fly kites."

Tibby stared at her. "*You* flew kites?"

Aunt Evelyn nodded. "With Veronica, when she was a girl."

Tibby didn't know what to say.

"Come on," Aunt Evelyn said. "Louie here could use some fresh air." She snapped a leash on the crippled dog.

"But I have homework," Tibby said, "and my project."

"You can do your homework after we get home," Aunt Evelyn said. "And you and Katie deserve a night off from that project. I'll call her mother."

"No," Tibby said quickly. "I will."

Tibby went up to her room to make the call. The Milners didn't have a phone, of course, so she just talked to the dial tone. She spoke nice and loud, so Aunt Evelyn would hear.

"Okay, Katie," she said. "I'll see you tomorrow."

She hoped Mrs. Milner wouldn't worry too much. And she hoped the Lord would understand.

The farm had changed hands since Veronica was a girl, but the new owner said they could fly the kite anyway.

"I'm afraid I can't run the way I used to," Aunt Evelyn said, so she and Lou Grant stood watching while Tibby ran to get the kite in the air. The long dragon tail finally streaked across the sky, and Tibby wished Veronica were there to see it.

"See?" Aunt Evelyn said in the car on the way home. "I think you and I can get along pretty well by ourselves."

The next night Tibby went back to meeting, and the prayers for Veronica's return seemed more fervent than ever.

Aunt Evelyn never said anything, but it looked like she was settling in for a long stay. More and more of her possessions showed up in Veronica's house every day. Aunt Evelyn brought her own patchwork quilt for the bed in the guest room, she set up her photographs on the piano in the living room, and she asked Tibby to help her move furniture in the den to make room for her rocker.

"Isn't this nice?" she asked Tibby when they'd finished. "Now it looks more like a home and less like a picture in a magazine."

Tibby accepted the changes without complaint. She knew everything would change back again once Veronica came home to stay.

In the meantime she hoped the Lord noticed how patient she was.

Aunt Evelyn started coming into her room every night. Once or twice she even leaned over Tibby's bed as if she might like to kiss her. But Tibby buried herself in the covers, so there wasn't anything to kiss.

"School will be getting out in a couple of weeks," Aunt Evelyn said on one of her nightly visits. "Shouldn't you be finishing your project?"

"I guess so." Tibby felt uncomfortable. What would she do if Veronica didn't come home by the time school got out?

"Bolivia is such a big topic. Are you drawing posters, writing reports, or what?"

"Uh-huh," Tibby said.

"What?"

"We're drawing posters, writing reports, everything."

"Goodness, I'd like to see this project. Will I be able to see it before you turn it in?"

"I don't think so," Tibby said. "We probably won't get it done until the night before it's due."

Aunt Evelyn nodded. "That sounds just like Veronica. Working right up to the deadline."

Tibby smiled.

"But I could go over to Katie's house and see it there," Aunt Evelyn said.

Tibby stopped smiling.

"Or maybe I should just wait and see it after it's been graded."

Tibby smiled again. The project could get lost at school.

"I'm sure you'll get a good grade, after all this work," Aunt Evelyn said. "I just hope Katie's mother knows how much I appreciate her letting you work at her house every night. Maybe I should call her."

"Oh, I wouldn't do that."

"Why not?"

Tibby thought fast. "She's hard of hearing, and she doesn't like to talk on the phone. The cheesecake was enough. She really liked the cheesecake."

Aunt Evelyn looked pleased. "I do make a tasty

cheesecake, even if I do say so myself," she said. "But I'd like to do more. I think Katie and her family are having a wonderful influence on you. Ever since you've been working on this project, you've been so much calmer and so much — "

"Maybe I could take them some flowers or something." Mrs. Milner would love flowers. She'd thank Tibby and she'd praise the Lord and then she'd put them in the center of the picnic table where everyone would admire them.

"That's a lovely idea, Tibby," Aunt Evelyn said. "I'll get some flowers."

Then she swooped down and kissed Tibby before she had a chance to pull up the covers.

It was Aunt Evelyn's turn to have the bridge club luncheon at her house the next day, so she didn't have time to get flowers. Dinner was late, too, and Tibby had to hurry to get ready for meeting. She was looking for her shoes — the plain black ones that she always wore to meeting — when the phone in her room rang. It was Patsy Franklin.

"Whatcha doing?" Patsy asked.

"Not much." Tibby held the phone to her shoulder while she groped under the bed for her left shoe.

"Did you see Sara's face today when Mrs. Crawley — "

Tibby found the shoe and slipped it on. "Listen, Patsy, I can't talk right now. I'm in kind of a hurry."

"Well, *excuse me!* I wouldn't want to interrupt your *busy* schedule."

Tibby didn't say anything.

"You know what, Tibby? You're getting to be a real *bore*. You never smart off anymore, and you never go anywhere or do anything. You've lost it, kid."

Tibby knew she meant her flair, and she felt sorry, for just a moment. But then she remembered she had something better. She had the Lord. And she had the Milners. And soon she would have Veronica, too.

But the next day she came home from school and found Aunt Evelyn smiling in that strange old way, with the gold glittering in the back of her mouth.

"Are you going over to Katie's again tonight?" Aunt Evelyn asked.

"Uh-huh." Tibby headed up the stairs.

"Well, tell Mrs. Carlson I said hello." Aunt Evelyn paused. "I finally met her today, and she seemed like a lovely woman."

Tibby stopped on the stairs, with her back to Aunt Evelyn.

"I decided to take some flowers over to her myself today," Aunt Evelyn said. "I looked up the Carlsons' address and found it on Riverview Drive, just like you said. When Mrs. Carlson came to the door, I told her how much I appreciated everything she's done for you, but she didn't seem to understand a thing I was saying. At first I thought she couldn't hear me. So I shouted."

Aunt Evelyn waited for this to sink in.

"Then I realized that she heard me just fine. And I was the one who didn't understand."

Tibby wondered what she would do.

"You've been going to those prayer meetings, haven't you." There was no question in her voice, only disappointment. "And I thought we were beginning to trust each other."

Tibby had to stay home that night. She prayed and praised by herself, but it wasn't the same.

CHAPTER 18

VERL and Esther were waiting for her on the wooded path by the river in the morning.

"You missed another meeting last night," Esther said. "That's not the way to get the Lord to listen."

"Did your aunt want you to go somewhere again?" Verl asked.

"No, she just wanted me to stay home. She says I can't come to meetings anymore." They might as well know the truth.

"Why not?" Esther asked. "Why'd she change her mind?"

Tibby shrugged. She didn't want to tell them about Katie Carlson.

"I'm glad you didn't disobey her," Verl said.

"We prayed for you anyway," Esther said. "Did your mama come home yet?"

"No," Tibby said.

Esther nodded wisely. "You can't rush the Lord," she said. "I've been waiting for my Barbie doll ever since I can remember."

Tibby thought the Lord should put a higher priority on her mother than Esther's Barbie doll, but she didn't say so.

"I guess this means you won't be coming anymore," Verl said.

Tibby shrugged. "Maybe I'll think of something."

Verl shook his head. "You must obey her. 'Honor thy father and thy mother.' " He raised his hand to meet her protest. "And in this case, I think the Lord meant thy aunt, too."

"Don't worry, Tibby," Esther said. "We'll still pray for you."

All day Tibby tried to think of a way to go to meeting that night. She didn't think Aunt Evelyn would believe any stories about having to go to the library or Patsy Franklin's house or the mall. But maybe she could sneak out, somehow.

Aunt Evelyn made it clear, though, that there would be no sneaking. After Tibby got home from school, the woman checked up on her every fifteen minutes. Even when Tibby was in her room doing homework.

She knocked on Tibby's door and poked her head inside.

"You're not planning any trips to Bolivia, are

you?" she asked, and smiled. She evidently thought that was funny.

Verl was waiting on the path again in the morning, and he had a note from his mother. It was written in pencil on yellow lined paper.

> *My deer child,*
> *I am so sorry to heer that you canot come to meeting any more. But you must obay your aunt. Remember that we love you and we are praying for you. Your mother will come and she will beleve.*
>
> *Your loveing freind,*
> *Judith Milner*

Tibby read the note again and again throughout the day. Her eyes kept stopping on the words *Your mother will come and she will beleve.* She held on to those words and played them over and over in her head.

She pictured Veronica and Mrs. Milner as good friends, the kind she had seen in the barn every night. They'd sit together and talk and laugh and pray together. And they'd both love Tibby.

Then, on her way home from school, it suddenly occurred to Tibby — or maybe the Lord told her — why Veronica hadn't come. Why she couldn't come. Tibby had been praying for the wrong thing. Or maybe it was the right thing, but for the wrong reason.

Tibby had been praying for Veronica to come

home, just because she wanted a mother. She had forgotten about Veronica's soul.

Veronica had to come home to believe in the Lord. Even the Ouija board had told her to B-E-L-I-E-V-E. But how could she if she'd never heard of the Believers? Tibby had to tell her.

So Tibby ran the rest of the way home and found, next to the phone in the den, the telephone number where Veronica was staying in Columbus.

"Hello?" Aunt Evelyn called. "Is that you, Tibby? How was your day?"

"Okay. But I've got a lot of homework." She hurried up to her room and dialed Veronica's number. An operator said she wasn't there, so Tibby left a message for her to call back.

Veronica called around four-thirty. "What's up, Tib?" she asked. "Is something wrong?"

"No, I just wanted to tell you about the Believers."

"You called to tell me about a rock group?"

"The Believers aren't a rock group. They're people right here in Seneca, and they pray for miracles."

"Miracles?"

"Yeah. One man needed money, and everybody prayed. Then he went home and found a five-hundred-dollar bill in his Bible."

"Five hundred bucks in a Bible!" Veronica laughed. "That's my kind of miracle!"

"It really happened," Tibby said. "I was there.

And there have been other miracles, too. A mother prayed, and her dead baby just started breathing. Somebody else prayed, and his car moved off the railroad tracks right before a train hit it. And another guy — "

"Really?" Veronica had stopped laughing, and Tibby could tell she was impressed. "You were there? You heard all this stuff?"

"Uh-huh. You should come, too."

"Hmmm. That's an interesting idea, Tib. Let me check into it."

Tibby felt the power of the Lord rushing through her. Veronica would come home soon, and it would be the best homecoming yet. Because this time she would stay. Stay and believe.

Verl waited for her on the path almost every morning. Sometimes Esther was with him, and she always asked about Tibby's mother and told how everyone was still praying for her return. But Verl never said much, except maybe to tell her the name of a bird or a flower they saw as they walked along. Tibby didn't know why he kept coming, but she was glad he did. He was her link with the Lord.

It was hard to keep praying by herself, without the singing and clapping and smiling faces in the barn. At night she closed her eyes and tried to pretend she was still there, with Verl on one side of her and Mrs. Milner on the other, and everyone praying together. But her mind would wander. To old TV shows, homework assignments, kids she used to know, Ouija boards.

She tried to bring her mind back to the barn by concentrating on the details: the way Brother Ralph's voice rose and fell as he told of new miracles, the way everyone lined up for his blessing, the money they poured into baskets.

Tibby thought of those baskets with shame. She had never put anything in them. Not one cent.

No wonder the Lord hadn't answered her prayers.

She had to give. But what, and to whom? Even if she had money, she couldn't take it to meeting. Not with Aunt Evelyn checking on her all the time.

Then Tibby thought of something to give. It wasn't much, but it was better than nothing. And she would give it to Verl, her link with the Lord.

She would give him the book she'd bought in Washington about Indian relics. She knew how much Verl liked knowing the names of flowers and birds. He'd want to know about the Indians, too.

In the morning Tibby took the book with her on the wooded path. She waited at their usual spot, but Verl didn't come. Where was he? Verl had missed mornings before, but this was a special morning, her chance to give, and the least he could do was show up.

Off in the distance, she heard St. Agnes' first bell, and she had to leave. With the weekend coming, and with Aunt Evelyn watching her every move, she knew she wouldn't be able to give him the book until Monday morning, at the very earliest. And Monday was such a long time away.

If only the Lord would give her the opportunity to see Verl — to offer her gift — over the weekend.

CHAPTER 19

THE Lord dropped the opportunity in Tibby's lap Saturday morning. Aunt Evelyn had spilled a glass of orange juice on the kitchen floor and was cleaning up the mess when Lou Grant started whining to go outside.

"Oh, Louie," Aunt Evelyn said. "You pick the most inconvenient times."

"I can take him," Tibby offered.

Aunt Evelyn looked at Tibby, then at the dog, and finally at the juice on the floor.

"Why not?" she finally said. "You probably both need some time without me hovering over you."

Tibby ran upstairs to get the book.

She thought she would have to walk slowly to accommodate the three-legged dog, but Lou Grant had a brisk, if lopsided, gait. They were soon at the blue trailer.

Naomi was outside playing, with Jeremiah and Ezekiel. They stopped to fuss over Lou Grant.

"What happened to him?" Jeremiah asked. "Where's his other leg?"

"I don't know," Tibby said.

"You don't know!" The children were amazed.

"He's been like this as long as I've known him," Tibby said, but she could see that didn't satisfy these little kids. She should ask Aunt Evelyn about Lou Grant's missing leg. "Is Verl around?"

"He's at Mr. Solimano's lot," Naomi said. "He took Esther with him." She pouted. "I had to stay here."

Tibby thought about stopping to see Mrs. Milner. She'd probably hug her and call her honey. But she might send Tibby back, before she had a chance to offer her gift.

So Tibby walked on. As she approached Solimano's lot, she could see Verl kneeling over the flowers in the circular garden and Esther sitting in the grass under the fruit trees. They didn't see her yet, and she looked beyond them, up the hill that led to the old Indian campground. She hadn't been back there since Aunt Evelyn went to see Mrs. Carlson. She wanted to go there now and follow its paths and imagine its people and join her prayers with theirs.

But first she had to give Verl the book.

"Hey, Verl!" she called.

"Look!" Esther cried. "It's Tibby!"

"Does your aunt know you're here?" Verl asked.

Tibby shrugged.

"She doesn't," Verl answered himself. "You'd best be going."

"Why'd you come, Tibby?" Esther asked. "Why'd you come? And who's the dog? Did you know he's missing a leg?"

Tibby nodded and grinned. "I've got something for Verl." She wished she'd brought something for Esther, too.

"What is it, Tibby? What is it?"

Tibby kept the book tucked inside her sweatshirt. "It's a surprise."

"A surprise?" Verl looked interested, but then he caught himself. "You're not supposed to be here."

"I'm not leaving. Not until I give you this."

He was just as stubborn. "Well, I'm not taking it." He motioned to a pile of onions on the ground. "I've got work to do."

"I'm not stopping you." Tibby sat down to wait.

Verl dug a hole about six inches deep and plopped an onion into it.

"That seems pretty stupid," Tibby said. "Planting onions in with the flowers."

Verl laughed. "These aren't onions. They're gladiola bulbs, and they'll be real pretty, come July." Then he remembered that he was angry with Tibby. "You're not supposed to be here," he said again.

"But I am."

He didn't say anything else. He just kept digging and plopping.

Esther grinned at Tibby. "I've never seen a three-legged dog before," she said. "Is he yours?"

"No," Tibby said, "he belongs to my aunt."

"The one who made the cheesecake?"

Tibby nodded, and Esther knelt down to pet Lou Grant. "Why'd you come?" she asked again. "Is your mama home?"

"No, but I know she'll come, really soon. I figured out what was keeping her."

"What?"

"I was praying wrong. I was praying for her to come home. But now I'm praying for her to *believe*."

Esther nodded. "That's a good idea. I think the Lord'll like that."

"I don't know why it took me so long to figure it out," Tibby said. "Even the Ouija board said she had to believe."

"The wee-gee board?" Esther asked. "What's a wee-gee board?"

"It's a game that tells about the future. It told my mother to believe. And it told me to help her."

"Do you think it could tell me how to get a Barbie doll?"

"I don't know," Tibby said. "Maybe."

Verl finally placed the last bulb in the last hole and covered it with dirt and wood chips.

"Do you want your surprise now?" Tibby asked him.

But Verl still ignored her. He took his trowel and hoe back to the shed, then double-checked the lock on the shed door before he went up to Mr. Solimano's back door. He and Mr. Solimano talked for a few minutes, with Verl gesturing toward the circular flower bed and Mr. Solimano nodding.

"What's the surprise?" Esther asked. "What is it?"

"You'll see," Tibby said.

"But what if he doesn't take it?"

"He will."

Verl came back. "If I take this, you'll go home."

Tibby nodded. "Right away."

"And you'll never, ever disobey your aunt again."

Tibby crossed her fingers. "Never."

"All right," he sighed. "Let me have it."

Tibby pulled out the book.

"Oh, no," Esther said.

"What's wrong?" Tibby asked.

"It's a book," Verl said softly.

"What's wrong with a book?"

Verl hesitated, but Esther piped up: "We need only one book, the Lord's book."

"This is just a paperback," Tibby said. "It's not in competition with the Bible."

"He still can't take it," Esther said. "Can you, Verl?" But Verl looked at the book as if he'd like to.

"Can't you just look at it?" Tibby asked.

"My hands are dirty," Verl said.

"So wipe them off."

He spat on both palms and wiped them on his jeans. Then he took the book gently, as if it might break. At first he just held the book in both hands, looking at the cover picture of a clay pot.

"You shouldn't look at a book," Esther warned.

128

But Verl opened it and turned the pages slowly, absorbed in the pictures and captions. Then he came to the photograph of a prayer stick.

"That's it," he said, with a pleased look. "That's what I found." But the look darkened as he read the caption. "Oh, no."

"What's wrong?" Tibby asked.

"It says here that the Kickapoo Indians used this when they prayed to their gods."

"Their *gods?*" Esther's voice was shrill.

"So?" Tibby didn't understand.

"They used the stick to honor gods." Verl paused. "False gods."

"You have to destroy it," Esther said.

"What?" Tibby almost laughed. "We're talking about *Indians,* a long time ago."

"Remember how Moses destroyed the golden calf, Verl," Esther said. "You'll have to do the same."

Verl looked at his sister.

"You should *burn* that prayer stick." Esther looked nervously toward the sky. "And you'd better do it quick, before the Lord sends His wrath."

Verl bit his lip, hesitating, and Tibby looked to the top of the hill, almost expecting to see an old chief rising in protest.

"You can't destroy the prayer stick," she said. "It doesn't belong to you. You said so yourself." Tibby thought of the young brave praying before his first hunt. And the girl waiting for her mother to return.

"I know." Verl blinked rapidly. "But it was used to honor false gods."

"You're crazy, Verl. You really are."

"He's not crazy," Esther said. "He has to follow the way of the Lord. Don't you, Verl?"

Verl didn't say anything, and Tibby snatched back the book. But she couldn't take back what he knew.

CHAPTER 20

BROTHER Ralph was waiting with Verl on the path by the river on Monday morning, only Tibby didn't recognize the preacher at first without his white suit. She'd never imagined Brother Ralph wearing anything else, or doing anything else but preaching. She wondered why he'd come.

She looked at Verl, whose eyes were on the ground. Maybe he'd told Brother Ralph about the book. Maybe Brother Ralph was mad.

But Brother Ralph smiled, really big. "My child," he said, holding out both hands to grasp Tibby's. "How we have missed you. And how we have prayed for you."

Tibby heard, in his wonderful voice, the sound of love and the sound of the Lord.

"And you, child, have you been praying?"

Tibby nodded.

"Praise the Lord for that!" Brother Ralph closed his eyes and raised his face to heaven for a moment. Then he opened his eyes and looked at Tibby. "I believe you are a special child, Tibby, and the Lord has special plans for you. But you know it's not the same to pray by yourself. It is much more blessed to pray with others."

Tibby nodded again. She'd found that out, all right. It was too hard to concentrate.

Brother Ralph smiled warmly. "Did you know that the Lord talks to me?"

"Yes," Tibby said. She'd heard him tell of his conversations with God.

"He talked to me when I first saw Seneca from a Greyhound bus two years ago. 'Ralph,' the Lord said, 'the people here are crying out for your help.' I got off that bus right then and there, and I've been helping the people of Seneca ever since."

Tibby nodded.

"The Lord also talked to me the first night you came to meeting. 'Ralph,' the Lord said, 'look at that child in the front row with the Milners. She's bringing you a special challenge, Ralph.' And I said to the Lord, 'I'm ready, Lord, I'm ready.' But I didn't know what that challenge would be until Verl's father told me last night."

Tibby glanced over at Verl. She wondered what the special challenge was, and how Verl's father knew about it. But Verl kept his eyes on the ground.

"Verl, my boy, you have done your duty,"

Brother Ralph said. "This child and I need to be alone, for the Lord to work His wonders."

Verl hesitated, looking first at Tibby, then at the preacher. "Yes, sir," he finally said, and left.

Brother Ralph watched Verl go, then turned back to Tibby. "Come with me, child," he said, leading her off the path, down the hill, and into the brush by the river. Tibby thought, for just a moment, of the drunks and perverts that Mrs. Mendelson was always screaming about. But Brother Ralph began humming "Amazing Grace," and she knew she didn't have to worry. Brother Ralph wasn't drunk, and he certainly wasn't a pervert. He was a man of the Lord.

Still humming, Brother Ralph let go of Tibby's hand and stepped onto the soft riverbank. He turned and placed his hands on her head, the same way he did the first night she went to the barn, and she felt that same surge of the Lord's love. "Oh, the Lord is in our presence, I can tell!" Brother Ralph said. Then he lowered his hands to her shoulders. "And He will surely guide us today."

Tibby waited for something wonderful — maybe a miracle — to happen.

Brother Ralph bent to gather river water in his cupped hands. Then he spun around and threw the water at Tibby's face.

She jumped back in surprise.

"Out, Satan, out!" he shouted.

Was the devil here? Tibby looked around.

Brother Ralph brought his face down in front of

Tibby's and looked at her with blazing eyes. "I know you are there, Satan, and I'll not let you go this time!"

Was the devil in *her*? Was that what he meant? She opened her mouth, but only a squeaking gasp came out.

"Out, I say, out!" He grasped her head between his big hands and squeezed until it hurt. "You thought you'd fool me this time, coming in the form of an innocent child! *An innocent child!*" He laughed. "Born to a drug addict and raised by a *TV reporter!*" He spat out those last words, full of contempt. "But you gave yourself away when you spoke through the Ouija board. And now I command you to let this child go!"

Tibby struggled to free herself. But the preacher's hands were too strong.

"There's no use trying to get away, Satan," he said, laughing. "I've got you now!" He forced Tibby down on the muddy riverbank, then grabbed her by the back of her neck and pushed her face into the water. He held her there for just a second, then brought her up for air.

"Out, Satan, out!" he shouted and pushed her face down in the water again. He dunked her again and again. All the time he kept shouting, but Tibby couldn't understand the words. She could only sputter and swallow and struggle for air.

Finally he stopped, and she lay gasping in the mud.

"Hallelujah!" Brother Ralph raised his hands to

heaven. "We beat him again, Lord!" He looked down at Tibby. "Are you all right, child? That old devil fought us good and hard, but the Lord whupped him!"

Tibby still couldn't speak.

"And now I hear Him talking to you. Can you hear Him, child? The Lord's calling your name! Listen!"

Tibby raised her head and pretended to listen. Then she heard it: *"Tibby!"*

"Can't you hear Him, child?" Brother Ralph asked. "Can't you?"

"Tibby!" It was a woman's voice. "Tibby! Tibby!"

It was Aunt Evelyn, standing at the top of the hill.

"I'm coming, Lord!" Tibby yelled, and ran up the hill to her.

Aunt Evelyn gasped when she saw her. "What happened?"

But Tibby couldn't answer. She could only cry.

Aunt Evelyn put her arms around her, as muddy as she was, and murmured, "Oh, my poor child."

CHAPTER 21

TIBBY was still shaking as she walked down the path with Aunt Evelyn. She kept looking back, wondering if Brother Ralph would come after them.

"He won't come," Aunt Evelyn said. "He wouldn't dare."

Tibby looked up at her face, with the hard lines and the set jaw. Aunt Evelyn was right. Nobody would come after a face like that.

When they reached the fence, Tibby wondered how the old woman would get over it. Maybe she should help her.

But Aunt Evelyn didn't need help. "Good thing I wore slacks today," she said as she put one foot, then the other, on the crossbars and eased herself over to the other side, as if she'd climbed this fence before. Tibby wondered about that, just as she wondered how Aunt Evelyn had known to come looking for her.

But she forgot everything when they came around the house and saw a familiar red head waiting in the driveway. Tibby stopped.

Aunt Evelyn kept on walking. She held out her hand to Verl, and they talked a few minutes, as if they were old buddies. Then Aunt Evelyn went inside.

Verl came to meet Tibby.

"I'm sorry," he said.

"You should be."

"I didn't know what was going to happen."

Tibby didn't say anything.

"But," he tried to explain, "Esther told my father about the prayer stick and the Ouija board. He said maybe you were possessed. By the devil."

"Do you think I'm possessed?" She wondered if his mother thought that, too.

He hesitated. "I don't know what to think. Esther got a bad earache last night, and my father said it was because of what she'd heard."

"Do you think I'm possessed." It wasn't a question anymore.

"I don't know, but my father said I should take Brother Ralph to you." He looked at her. "I had to do it, Tibby. My father said."

Of course he had to do it. *Honor thy father and thy mother.*

*   *   *

Aunt Evelyn never asked exactly what happened at the riverbank. She seemed to understand that Tibby didn't want to talk about it. She did ask once, though, whether Tibby had seen Verl since then.

"No, and I don't want to," Tibby said.

"You mustn't think too harshly of him, Tibby," she said. "He's a very confused boy, and he just tried to do what's right."

Tibby stared at her. Wasn't this the same woman who kept warning her how dangerous the Believers were?

"You don't know what happened," she said.

"No, I don't," Aunt Evelyn admitted, "but I've got a pretty good idea. And I *do* know what Verl did."

Tibby wondered, for just a moment, if Verl had gotten in trouble for going to Aunt Evelyn. But she didn't try to find out.

She wanted to forget all about the Believers. She filled her days with school, homework, and television. Aunt Evelyn still asked her to play Scrabble and walk Lou Grant, and they flew the kite one more time, but mostly Aunt Evelyn just left Tibby alone. Tibby understood that she had her old freedoms back. But she didn't go anywhere or do anything. Just school, homework, and television.

She watched lots of television. She watched cartoons, Cubs games, old movies, quiz shows, talk shows, soap operas, anything. And she did it all without thinking. If she watched enough TV, maybe she'd never have to think about anything else, ever again.

Once she saw a soap opera with the world's longest kiss. That kind of kissing used to embarrass Tibby — even when no one else was in the room — so she'd change the channel or turn off the TV.

But this time she watched the kiss, fascinated. The man and woman had their mouths open and their jaws working so it looked like they were trying to eat each other. She wondered if Veronica had ever kissed somebody like that. Probably not. She'd once told Tibby that she never met a man who could hold her interest for very long.

But maybe you didn't have to be interested to kiss a man like that. Just like maybe you didn't have to live with the kid that was supposed to be your daughter. And maybe you didn't have to love a kid just because you hugged her and called her honey.

You sure wouldn't love her if the devil was in her.

Sometimes at night, when the lights were out, her mind drifted back to the yellow barn and all the singing and praising there. And she remembered, with a special ache, Mrs. Milner.

The Believers, all of them, had been so good. And so close to God.

But then she remembered the riverbank and Brother Ralph's eyes blazing at the devil within her. If those people were so good and so close to God, how could Brother Ralph have been so wrong?

He was wrong, wasn't he?

She couldn't think about it. She had to crush out those thoughts and think about something else.

Every television show had a mother or a preacher or a good friend. She had to think about something completely different.

Like Indians. It was safe to think about Indians.

If the Indians had camped on Solimano's lot, maybe they had stopped at other spots along the river, too. On Saturday she went to a small park that ran along a section of the river, and she looked there for signs of Indian life. She followed a weedy trail, past the tennis courts and playground equipment, into the thick overgrowth, where she discovered a lot of things: nettles that clung to her socks, sticky vines that grew to her armpits, and the old stone foundation of a small building.

She also discovered poison ivy.

The itchy, burning rash spread up her arms and legs.

"Don't scratch," Aunt Evelyn said. "That'll only make it worse."

But Tibby couldn't help it. She had to scratch. And the itching and burning did get worse. It got so bad that Aunt Evelyn let her stay home from school a couple of days, and she smeared a pink lotion on Tibby four times a day.

The lotion felt cool and smooth, and Aunt Evelyn's fingers were gentle.

One evening Aunt Evelyn came into Tibby's room, just when it was time for the news to begin. After she smeared the lotion on Tibby's arms and legs, she stayed and watched the show. Near the end, the anchorman talked about the governor closing the savings-and-loan associations in Ohio while the screen showed people waiting in long lines. Tibby looked for Veronica, but didn't see her.

"She was on several times, when you were . . . uh . . . away. But I don't think you ever saw the tape." Aunt Evelyn spoke carefully, as if the words might break.

"I could look at it now," Tibby said, just as carefully.

So Aunt Evelyn got the tape, and Tibby put it in the VCR. The first thing that came on was a commercial for rental cars.

Aunt Evelyn took the remote-control switch and fast-forwarded past the commercials. "I love doing this," she said. "It's like throwing popcorn at the screen, only you don't have a mess to clean up afterward."

Tibby thought back to the night in Chicago, when she and Veronica had thrown popcorn at the TV screen. She didn't remember anyone cleaning up the mess.

They watched the tape — Veronica had been on four times — and the next night Tibby took the poison ivy lotion into the guest room to watch the news with Aunt Evelyn. They sat on the couch, with Lou Grant between them, and Tibby remembered to ask about his missing leg.

"I'm not sure exactly," Aunt Evelyn said. "I think

he was in some kind of train accident. Or maybe it was a bus. You'd have to ask Veronica."

"Why would she know?"

"She's the one who brought him home," Aunt Evelyn said. "It was before she went to the network. She was covering a story, and there was a little dog that had been hurt. They were going to put him to sleep but Veronica said no." She smiled at the memory. "Veronica's always had a soft spot for animals in trouble."

Then how did you end up with him? Tibby wanted to ask, but she was afraid of the answer.

Aunt Evelyn seemed to know the question. "Of course, a dog couldn't fit into her schedule, so after a while she asked me if I'd like to take him." She smiled at that memory, too. "I guess I've got a soft spot, too."

"But that left you with the responsibility," Tibby pointed out.

"I don't mind," Aunt Evelyn said, scratching Lou Grant behind the ear. "He's worth it."

Veronica came on the TV just then, and she talked in her clipped television voice about failing public confidence.

"Oh, dear," Aunt Evelyn said. "This story could go on and on."

Veronica came home the next night. She didn't call ahead, so it was a surprise. The best kind of surprise. Tibby almost praised His holy name.

"What about the savings and loans?" Aunt Evelyn asked. "Aren't they still closed?"

"Terry's going to cover it," Veronica said. "I convinced Mel that I had a better story."

Oh. She was just stopping by to change suitcases.

"Right here in Seneca."

"In Seneca?"

Veronica nodded. "Tibby told me about it."

Tibby was as surprised as Aunt Evelyn.

"I did some checking, Tib, and everything you told me was true." Veronica hugged her. "You're getting to be a real reporter!"

"What's the story?" Aunt Evelyn asked. Tibby wanted to know, too.

"The Believers."

Tibby and Aunt Evelyn looked at each other.

"Haven't you heard about them?" Veronica asked. "The religious fanatics?"

"Oh, yes," Aunt Evelyn said vaguely, with her eyes still on Tibby, "I think I read something about them in the paper."

"Tibby's even met some of them," Veronica said. "Right, Tib?"

Tibby nodded. Suddenly, for the first time since Brother Ralph tried to drown the devil in her, Tibby wanted to talk about the Believers. She wanted to tell her mother everything — about the nights in the barn and the praying and the miracles and even the morning by the riverbank. And there would be time, now that Veronica was here to work on a story.

"So I thought maybe Tibby and I could work on this together."

A small voice in the back of Tibby's head worried. *But I thought you said you liked to work alone. Without other people.*

Veronica smiled. "This could be a real mother-daughter project."

A real mother-daughter project. It sounded so good. Tibby silenced the voice and accepted the miracle.

CHAPTER 22

TIBBY wanted to tell Veronica about everything that had happened. But Veronica didn't have time that night. She had to make a lot of phone calls.

In the morning Veronica wanted to walk over to the barn. "The camera crew won't be here until this afternoon," she said, setting down her coffee cup. "But I like to meet people ahead of time, on my own. I've found that I get better interviews in the end if they feel like I'm their friend."

"Can I go with you?" Tibby asked.

Veronica smiled. "You'd better. I'm counting on you to introduce me to people."

"Then you'll have to wait until this afternoon," Aunt Evelyn said.

"Why?"

"Tibby has school."

"It wouldn't hurt to miss a day, would it, Tib?"

"Not a bit." Tibby grinned.

"But she's missed a lot already," Aunt Evelyn said. "There was the trip to Washington and the poison ivy and the day she went in late because of — "

"So what? She'd learn more in a morning with me than she would in a week of school."

"That's not the point."

"Well, what *is* the point? Is this some kind of power struggle?"

Aunt Evelyn's mouth flapped open, then shut again.

"I just can't figure out what you want," Veronica said. "You're always calling, scolding me for staying away so long, telling me how much this kid needs me."

Tibby looked at Aunt Evelyn. Had she told Veronica that?

"Then when I finally get a chance to spend some time with her, you jump all over me."

Aunt Evelyn nodded. "I think I'll go upstairs and pack."

"Oh, stay." Veronica's voice got soft again, and Tibby guessed she wasn't mad after all. "There's no reason to get all huffy."

"I'm not getting huffy. I wanted to go home last night, when you got here, but it was so late that I — "

"All right, all right." Veronica waved her away. "Are you coming, Tib, or not?"

Tibby hesitated a moment, looking at Aunt Evelyn. "Sure," she said, following her mother out the door.

Outside, Veronica stretched her arms in the morning sun. "What a beautiful day," she said. "Is the church far from here?"

"Church?"

"You know, the Believers."

"Oh, they meet in a barn, just on the other side of St. Agnes," Tibby said. "I always walk."

Veronica smiled. "I can't tell you how long it's been since I've walked through the old neighborhood."

Tibby thought about taking her mother down the wooded path, but Veronica evidently wanted to see the old neighborhood from the front, not the back.

As they walked, Veronica pointed out where she'd played or visited when she was a kid. Tibby knew she'd never walk by one of those big old houses again without thinking, *That's where Veronica got a candy apple every Halloween*, or, *That's where Veronica used to spend the night*.

When they reached the barn, it looked empty, but Veronica tested the door, and it was unlocked, so she stepped inside. Tibby hesitated. This was the place she'd been pushing from her thoughts ever since the morning by the riverbank. Even now, with Veronica ahead of her, she felt uneasy about who or what might be waiting inside.

"Come on, Tib," Veronica called from inside. "We don't have all day."

Tibby stepped inside and looked around quickly. In the dim light, she saw the yellow walls, the rows of benches, and the hanging microphone. Nothing else. She felt a little silly. What had she expected? The Lord God Almighty?

"God, what a dump," Veronica said, kicking at the dirt floor.

"It's different at night," Tibby said, "when there's music and everybody's shouting . . ."

"And reaching into their pockets for money to buy Brother Ralph another Mercedes," Veronica said.

"A Mercedes?"

"Sure," Veronica said. "I checked, and he's got three of them. The Lord's work is very profitable. He can afford to stick five hundred bucks in a Bible now and then. It's a good investment."

What? The miracles weren't real? But the car on the railroad tracks. And the baby.

"Speaking of Brother Ralph," Veronica said, "do you know where I can find him?"

"He'll be here tonight."

"But I want to talk to him before then. Where does he live?"

"I don't know."

Veronica sighed. "I was counting on you to know that sort of thing."

Tibby looked around. "I guess we could ask the Milners."

"Who are the Milners?"

"They're Believers. They're . . . real nice. And they live right near here."

"Great."

But Tibby wasn't sure it was great. She wasn't sure how Mrs. Milner felt about her anymore. Did she think the devil was in Tibby? If she did, Tibby didn't want to know.

When they went around the barn, Tibby expected to see some Milner kids playing outside, maybe leaping across the gully. But there was no one, and the old blue trailer stood alone.

"It looks abandoned," Veronica said. "Are you sure somebody lives here?"

"They did last week."

"Well, let's give it a try." Veronica hiked her skirt and jumped across the gully. She went to the trailer door and banged on it several times. No one answered. Out of the corner of her eye, Tibby thought she saw movement near a side window, but when she looked again, she didn't see anything.

"Are you sure this is where they live?" Veronica asked again.

"Maybe they're out selling Bibles," Tibby said.

"Do you know where?"

Tibby shook her head. Even if Verl and his father were selling Bibles, the others — Mrs. Milner and the little ones — should be here. They didn't have a car, and they never went anywhere except meetings.

Tibby remembered looking for Verl before, and

who had helped. "Maybe Mr. Solimano knows where they are," she said. "We could go over and ask."

"I can't afford to waste any more time," Veronica said.

Tibby was surprised. She didn't think they'd been wasting time.

"Mr. Solimano isn't far from here," Tibby said. "We could just check."

But it was farther than Tibby remembered. Or maybe it just seemed farther, with Veronica checking her watch every couple of minutes and always asking how much farther it was.

"There it is, up ahead," Tibby finally said, pointing to the small house.

"It's about time." Veronica looked at her watch again. "This Solimano fellow better know where everybody is."

Tibby ran ahead and rang the bell. Mr. Solimano came to the door. He frowned when he saw her.

"Verl's friend," he said.

"Do you know where he is?"

He shook his head. "He doesn't work here anymore. He quit, but not before he burned my best relic."

So Verl *had* destroyed the prayer stick.

"My wife, may she rest in peace, used to say, 'Sol, you shouldn't leave those relics out there. You should bring them in here, or give them to a museum.' But, no, I wanted to leave them there, where the Indians left them. I never thought anybody — least of all Verl — would hurt them."

Tibby was sorry about the prayer stick. But she couldn't hang around listening to this old man. Veronica was waiting. She had to go.

Mr. Solimano shook his head. "I never thought he was that kind of boy."

By the time Tibby came around the house again, Veronica was walking briskly down the road. Tibby ran to catch up with her.

"I'm sorry," she said.

"Forget it," Veronica said. But the tone of her voice wouldn't let Tibby forget it. Veronica had been counting on her, and she'd failed.

Neither of them said anything else until they came to St. Agnes. Then Veronica said, "You'd better stay here."

"Where?"

"Here. School. St. Agnes. God, Tib, don't act so dumb."

"But I don't have my bookbag. Or my books. I'll have to go home first."

"Forget it. You're staying here. *Now*."

CHAPTER 23

MRS. CRAWLEY sent Tibby to the office for a Parent Awareness Report.

Patsy was already there, waiting for Sister Josephine. "Keep-away with a second-grader's lunchbox," she explained. "What are you here for?"

"Coming late and without my books."

"Are you going to use that old line about some guy chasing you through the woods?"

"No, I'm going to say my mother didn't want me to come to school today, and when I finally managed to get here, she absolutely refused to let me bring my books."

Patsy grinned. "And I thought you'd lost your touch."

After school Tibby found the house key that Aunt Evelyn kept hidden in the flowerpot on the back porch. The phone was ringing when she unlocked the door. It was Aunt Evelyn.

"I'm glad I caught you," she said. "May I speak to Veronica, please?"

"She's not here."

"Oh? I thought you two were working together."

"Yeah, well."

Aunt Evelyn waited.

"She doesn't want me to help anymore. I screwed up."

Aunt Evelyn waited some more, but Tibby didn't say anything else.

"Well, I thought I'd invite you two over for dinner tonight," Aunt Evelyn finally said. "I'm making manicotti, with an old recipe I got from Veronica's mother."

"I don't know," Tibby said. "I'd better ask Veronica."

Aunt Evelyn laughed. "If I know Veronica, she won't think about food until the moment she's hungry. And there's no room service in that house."

Tibby remembered her first morning with Veronica, back in Chicago, when the only thing in the refrigerator had been a bottle of Cold Duck.

"Besides," Aunt Evelyn said, "Veronica and I need to talk, to get some things straightened out." She paused. "So why don't you come over after you finish your homework? I could use some help with this dough."

"But Veronica — "

"Just leave a note on the hall table," Aunt Evelyn said.

Tibby had been inside Aunt Evelyn's house only twice before, once right after the adoption and once right before they moved to Seneca. She remembered it as a small, crowded place, and she'd stayed away ever since. When Aunt Evelyn stopped sometimes to pick up the newspapers and check on things inside, Tibby always waited in the car.

When Tibby went inside today, she was surprised at how different the place seemed. Sure, it was still a lot smaller than Veronica's house, and the rooms didn't look like something in a magazine. But the kitchen had a dog door so Lou Grant could run in and out without whining, and the living room had a lot of interesting old photographs in picture frames, and fresh flowers in vases.

"Are these real?" Tibby asked, pointing to a bowl of yellow flowers on the kitchen table.

Aunt Evelyn nodded. "Fresh from the garden. They're Dutch tulips."

"You picked them today?"

"I pick some every day, to keep things looking fresh. It's nice to have them in the yard. In the winter, I have to buy flowers, and that gets expensive."

"You buy fresh flowers for *this* house?" It seemed silly to do that for an empty house.

"This is my home, Tibby. I just go to your house after school and at night."

"You still come here every day? I didn't know that."

Aunt Evelyn smiled. "I didn't want you to know your house was empty during the day. I thought it might give you ideas."

"Then why are you telling me now?"

Aunt Evelyn shook her head. "I don't know. Maybe I'm just a foolish old woman."

Tibby kneaded the pasta dough, grated the mozzarella, and chopped mushrooms and peppers for the manicotti sauce. She knew Aunt Evelyn would tell Veronica what a big help she'd been, and Tibby wanted — no, needed — to see that beautiful smile shining on her again.

But at 6:30, when the table was set and the manicotti was ready to come out of the oven, Veronica still hadn't called.

"Maybe she's trying to call your house," Aunt Evelyn said. "Why don't we wrap this in foil and take it over there?"

So they covered the manicotti and the salad and wrapped the garlic bread in aluminum foil. They took everything out to Aunt Evelyn's car. They were still in the driveway when Aunt Evelyn stopped the car and hurried back inside the house. She came out with her suitcase.

"I never had a chance to unpack today," she said, "and maybe it's just as well. I don't know how late Veronica will be."

When they got to Veronica's house, Aunt Evelyn

quickly slipped the manicotti and garlic bread into the oven while Tibby set the table. Then they sat down to wait.

At 8:00, when they still hadn't heard from Veronica, Aunt Evelyn took the manicotti out of the oven. "There's no use letting it dry out," she said. "We can save some for Veronica."

They both ate slowly, hoping Veronica would come. Aunt Evelyn sipped her wine and said, "This is very nice."

"It sure is," Tibby said.

But it wasn't.

When they couldn't drag out the process of eating any longer, they took their plates into the kitchen, where Tibby loaded the dishwasher and wiped the counters while Aunt Evelyn scrubbed at the crusty manicotti pan. Tibby noticed she was scrubbing with a vengeance, and her lower lip had turned white from biting.

"This really *was* a nice meal," Tibby said.

Aunt Evelyn looked at her in surprise, then smiled. "Maybe we should have this more often," she said. "After all, it was your grandmother's recipe."

Tibby was in bed by the time she heard Veronica's car in the driveway. She and Aunt Evelyn both hurried downstairs and were waiting when Veronica walked in the door.

"I don't believe those people," Veronica said. "It's like they never heard of a free press."

"What happened?"

"Nothing," Veronica said. "Nothing at all. They wouldn't talk to me, they wouldn't let me in their lousy meeting, and they said they'd sue me if a camera came near any of their damn Believers."

"Can't you do the story without cameras?" Tibby asked.

Veronica turned on her and laughed. "On television? I need *action*. I need hand clapping, Bible slapping, children dying—"

Aunt Evelyn glanced at Tibby. "You don't mean that."

"I went out on a limb with this story," Veronica said. "It was going to be my ticket to Washington."

"It still can be."

Veronica shook her head. "I told New York it would be really special, and they shuffled everyone around so I could do it. Now it's *got* to be special. Or they'll just think I'm another aging bimbo who can't tell a good story from a turkey."

Aunt Evelyn smiled. "No one thinks you're an aging bimbo."

"Oh, no? You should see the new girls they're hiring. Skinny, young, beautiful — and they've all got doctorates in political science."

"You're exaggerating," Aunt Evelyn said. "And I bet you haven't eaten. You always get cranky when you're hungry."

"I haven't eaten since this morning," Veronica admitted.

At last, Tibby could help. "Wait 'til you see what

we made for you," she said. "Manicotti! We can still heat it up, can't we?" Tibby looked at Aunt Evelyn, who nodded.

"Oh, don't bother," Veronica said. "I shouldn't be eating manicotti if I'm going to compete with all those skinny Ph.D.'s."

"But we made it especially for you."

"I said *don't bother*." And Veronica went upstairs to her room.

CHAPTER 24

VERONICA was gone by the time Tibby got up in the morning, and she didn't see her all day. She knew things probably weren't going well on the story. Brother Ralph would never talk to Veronica, and neither would any of his Believers.

It was all Tibby's fault. She never should have called Veronica and told her about the Believers.

Tibby and Aunt Evelyn were eating dinner alone again when the doorbell rang.

"Hush, Louie," Aunt Evelyn said to her barking dog. Then to Tibby: "Veronica must have forgotten her key. You let her in, and I'll set another place."

But it wasn't Veronica. It was Verl, with Esther limp in his arms.

"I can't wake her up," he said.

"What do you mean?" asked Aunt Evelyn, coming from the dining room.

"She had a real bad earache," he said, looking at his sister's flushed face. "We prayed for her, but . . ."

Aunt Evelyn stepped forward and put her hand on Esther's forehead. "She's burning up," she said. "Bring her in."

Verl carried Esther in and laid her on the sofa.

"What's her name?" Aunt Evelyn asked.

"Esther," Tibby said. "She's Verl's sister."

"Esther." Aunt Evelyn shook her shoulder. "Come on, Esther, wake up."

The little girl moaned softly. Aunt Evelyn looked at Verl.

"This child needs a doctor," she said. "Where are your parents?"

"Everyone went to meeting. They're praying for Esther right now. I was supposed to stay with her."

"And you took that opportunity to pull her out of her sick bed?" Aunt Evelyn looked at him sharply.

"Yes, ma'am."

Aunt Evelyn's look softened. "You did the right thing, Verl, the right thing." But she still looked worried. "I just wonder if anyone will treat her without her parents' permission."

"Can't *you* take care of her?" Verl asked. "Maybe give her some medicine?"

"No, Verl, I can't take care of her. I don't know what's wrong with her, and I wouldn't know where to begin." She nodded, as if to herself. "I'd better call Dr. Shelton." She headed for the phone in the kitchen.

"You can sit down," Tibby said, gesturing toward a chair, but Verl shook his head. He knelt by the couch and watched Esther's every breath.

Tibby didn't say anything else. But she wondered what made Verl go against God and his family by bringing Esther here. Verl, who always worried about honoring his father and mother and doing what Brother Ralph said was right. Verl, who destroyed the prayer stick.

She looked at Esther on the couch, though, and understood. This wasn't a piece of wood, used by Indians a long time ago. This was Esther, and she needed help, now.

Aunt Evelyn came back to the living room. "The doctor said to take her to the emergency room," she announced, "and he'll meet us there." She turned to Tibby. "Go get my purse, will you?"

Tibby started up the stairs, and Aunt Evelyn headed for the door. Only Verl — and Esther on the couch — didn't move.

"Well?" Aunt Evelyn said. "What are you waiting for? We need to hurry!"

"I don't know," Verl said, looking down at Esther. "Maybe I shouldn't do this. Maybe I should just pray."

Then why did you bring her here? Tibby wanted to ask. But she knew the answer.

"You can still pray, Verl," Aunt Evelyn said. "Just because you go to a doctor doesn't mean you have to stop praying."

"But my father says the Lord — "

"Maybe," Tibby heard herself say, "the Lord sent you here so you could get help for Esther."

Verl looked at her and nodded. But he still didn't move.

So Tibby asked what she had wanted to know for a long time: "Is this what happened to Dawn?"

He didn't say anything.

"Dawn?" Aunt Evelyn said. "Who's Dawn?"

Verl still didn't answer. But he picked up Esther and followed Aunt Evelyn out the door.

Tibby rushed out to the car with Aunt Evelyn's purse and started to get in, but Aunt Evelyn stopped her. "You'd better wait here," she said, "in case somebody comes looking for them."

"Who would come?"

"I don't know," Aunt Evelyn said, "but the doctor said the hospital will admit Esther if I take responsibility — and her parents aren't there to object. I don't want them to know about this and follow us. Not yet."

Tibby nodded and watched Aunt Evelyn's car back out of the driveway. She was just turning toward the house when another car pulled in. It was Veronica's.

"You'd think just one of those damn Believers would want to be on the tube," Veronica complained as she got out of the car. "I've got some pretty good stuff from the doctors and clergymen in town, but I need the other side. I need . . ."

Tibby knew what she needed. She needed something powerful and dramatic, something like a young Believer sneaking his sick sister into the hospital for medical treatment. Maybe an interview with him, and maybe an on-camera confrontation with his parents when they come rushing to the hospital to get their daughter.

Lord, it would make a great story. New York would be pleased, and so would Veronica. It would be the best mother-daughter project ever.

But if Veronica knew, pretty soon the Believers would know, and they'd go to the hospital. Maybe they'd get there in time to keep Esther out. Maybe . . .

Tibby thought of Verl, kneeling by the sofa.

But it would make such a good story. It might even be Veronica's ticket to Washington. And Tibby's ticket to that house in Virginia, where Veronica would come home every night.

Tibby knew she should help her mother. Kids always, always, always helped their mothers. Didn't they? Even the Ouija board had told Tibby to help Veronica. Hadn't it?

H-E-L-P-H-E-L-P-H-E-L-P-H-E-L-P-V

Maybe the *V* stood for Verl, not Veronica.

It didn't matter. Tibby couldn't listen to a Ouija board or Brother Ralph or Aunt Evelyn or even her own mother. She had to listen to herself.

*　*　*

Veronica kept talking about the Believers and their stubbornness while she ate dinner. Finally she noticed Aunt Evelyn's empty chair and the half-eaten plate of food.

"Where's Aunt E?" she asked.

"Oh, she went to the hospital . . . to see a friend," Tibby said.

"In the middle of dinner?"

"She was late." Suddenly Tibby wanted to stick her head in a toilet so she could throw up. She couldn't count the number of times she'd lied to Aunt Evelyn and teachers and sitters and social workers and foster mothers. But she'd never, ever, lied to Veronica before, and it made her sick.

Veronica accepted Tibby's story and went back to worrying about the Believers. "What about that family you know? The one we looked for in the trailer near the barn? Maybe one of them would talk to us if we could find them."

"I don't know," Tibby said. "I haven't seen any of them lately."

Then she excused herself and went upstairs to the bathroom.

Tibby stayed upstairs, waiting. She was waiting to hear how Esther was, and she was waiting for Veronica to find out.

Finally the phone rang. Veronica talked quietly for a few minutes, then slammed down the receiver and rushed up the stairs to Tibby's room. She flung the door open.

"How could you do this to me? You knew what this story meant to me!"

Tibby didn't try to explain.

Veronica put one hand on her hip and mimicked Tibby in a singsong voice: " 'Aunt Evelyn went to the hospital to visit a friend. She didn't finish her dinner because she was in such a hurry.' And I believed you! My own daughter! I had to wait for a *stranger* to call and tell me that my own aunt — "

Veronica stopped, evidently remembering what she had to do. She dove for the phone on Tibby's desk and dialed. "Hello, Tom? One of the Believers' kids got sick, and somebody took her to the hospital. Get the cameras over there right away, and I'll swing by the barn to see . . ."

While Veronica talked, Tibby slipped out of the room, down the stairs, and out to Veronica's car. She was waiting in the backseat when Veronica came racing out the front door.

"What are you doing here?" Veronica demanded.

Tibby just looked at her.

"Oh, what the hell, I don't have time to argue with you. But stay out of my way!"

Veronica didn't say anything while they sped toward the yellow barn. The car screeched to a stop, and Veronica jumped out. She ran to try the door. Tibby stayed in the car, but she could tell the barn was empty.

"Damn!" Veronica cried as she got back in the car. "They must be at the hospital! I must be the last person in town to know!"

Tibby held on to an armrest to keep from falling forward as Veronica threw the car into reverse.

Veronica spat out her rage at Tibby while they sped down streets and careened around corners. "When I think of all I've done for you — bailing you out of that stinking South Side apartment, buying that big old house, putting up with Aunt Evelyn — and this is the thanks I get! I suppose I should be glad you didn't give the story to another reporter." She looked in the rearview mirror at Tibby. "You didn't, did you?"

Tibby shook her head, bewildered. "I didn't do this to hurt you. They just needed some time."

Veronica didn't say anything.

The hospital parking lot was full when they got there. "There's the Mercedes," Veronica said. "Maybe I can still get something. . . ."

CHAPTER 25

THE hospital lobby was filled with crying, praising, praying people, and Tibby recognized many faces from her nights in the barn. Brother Ralph, in his white suit, was in the center of them all, shaking his fist and raging at a man with a stethoscope.

"That child is a child of God!" he cried. "You have no right to keep her here against the will of God!"

With a microphone in her hand and a cameraman behind her, Veronica pushed through the circle of Believers around Brother Ralph. Tibby stepped out of the way.

She looked around and saw Aunt Evelyn, off in a corner by herself. Tibby went over to her.

"How's Esther?" she asked.

"Not good," Aunt Evelyn said. "The doctor thinks it's meningitis, and they're giving her medicine intravenously, but it may be too late." She looked over at Brother Ralph, who had turned his rage on Veronica and the cameras. "The doctor says all we can do now is pray."

"But she's just a little kid," Tibby said.

Aunt Evelyn nodded.

"Where's Verl?"

"Upstairs, with his parents."

"Are they mad?"

Aunt Evelyn thought about it. "I don't think they're angry," she said, "but they think Verl was wrong, and they want to take Esther home."

"Can they?"

Aunt Evelyn shrugged. "The hospital is seeking a court order to keep her here. They said it was a good thing we got her here when we did — before they came," she said, nodding toward the Believers, "because it's easier to keep her here than to bring her in against her parents' wishes."

"But she still might die?"

Aunt Evelyn nodded.

When Brother Ralph and the Believers left, Veronica followed them out the door, with the cameras whirring behind her. In a few minutes she was back and came over to sit with Aunt Evelyn and Tibby.

"How's the little girl?" she asked.

"It doesn't look good," Aunt Evelyn said.

"I'm sorry." She put her hand on her aunt's. "Would you like to tell me — on camera — how you brought her here?"

Aunt Evelyn looked at Veronica. "I'd rather not," she said. "Do you mind?"

Veronica patted her hand. "No, that's all right," she said. "I understand." Then she got up and went over to talk to the nurse at the admitting desk.

Tibby watched in amazement. "Why didn't she get mad at you?" she asked Aunt Evelyn.

"Why should she?"

"She *exploded* when she found out I hadn't told her Esther was here."

Aunt Evelyn smiled. "That's because she was afraid she'd miss the story. But right now she has what she wants. She has Brother Ralph on tape arguing with the doctor. And that's better than an interview with her silly old aunt any day."

Tibby watched Veronica, showering the young nurse with beautiful smiles. The story. That's what was important to Veronica. Not living in her old hometown. Not some little kid dying. Not even her own little sweetie.

Just the story. And the chance of a minute or two on the network news.

Veronica went to Chicago the next day to finish taping her story. When she came home, she started packing.

"You have to go so soon?" Aunt Evelyn asked. "I thought you'd at least stay and find out what happens to Esther."

Veronica shook her head. "There's a hunger strike at the Iowa state prison," she said. "If something happens with that little girl, I can tag it on later, before the story goes on the air." They all knew she meant if Esther died.

"But we haven't really had a chance to talk," Aunt Evelyn said, "and we need to talk. About Tibby."

"Again?" Veronica sounded tired, and Tibby started to leave. She didn't want to hear what they would say.

"Don't go, Tibby." Aunt Evelyn turned back to Veronica. "It's hard for me to deal with problems that come up," she said.

"If it's hard, get a sitter," Veronica answered. "I told you that before."

"I don't want to get a sitter," Aunt Evelyn said. "I want to stay with Tibby myself. But I want to know that I have authority to do what I think is best."

"Authority!" Veronica started to laugh, but stopped when she saw her aunt's face. "Of *course*, you have the *authority* to do whatever you think is best." Just like that. "Satisfied?"

But Aunt Evelyn didn't smile. "Not completely," she said. "I want you to stay here and spend some time with your daughter."

Veronica put an arm around Tibby's shoulders. "Tibby understands," she said.

Tibby looked at the hand on her shoulder. It was as if the ugly words from the night before had never been spoken.

"Don't you, Tib?"

Tibby nodded. For the first time, she understood — completely — why Veronica had to leave. And why she couldn't keep her promises.

"I wish we had more time, Tib . . ."

"I know."

"Here." Veronica reached into her purse and pulled out a fifty-dollar bill. "Why don't you take some friends to a movie or something?"

Aunt Evelyn frowned. "That's a lot of money to give a child, for no reason at all."

But Tibby took the money, and knew the reason. Veronica couldn't give her anything else. Not when a story was waiting.

Veronica smiled. It was still a beautiful smile, and Tibby knew there would be times ahead when she would miss it. But right now it was nice to know that Veronica's smile was just a smile, and Tibby would be all right whether it shone on her or not.

CHAPTER 26

AFTER Veronica left the next morning, Aunt Evelyn told Tibby they were going to the 10:00 Mass. Together.

"My mother says I don't have to go to church on Sundays," Tibby said, smiling.

Aunt Evelyn smiled right back. "But your aunt says you do."

So Tibby went. Not because Veronica said Aunt Evelyn had the *authority*. She went because Aunt Evelyn wanted her to. And, well, because.

The Mass was quiet — no hand-clapping, no foot-stomping, and no miracles. But Tibby saw two kids from her class. And she saw Mrs. Mendelson.

When the Mass was over, Aunt Evelyn sat back in her pew and waited for the church to empty. Then she led Tibby up a side aisle to a statue of Jesus, surrounded on three sides by cushioned kneeling pads and rows of small candles in red glass cups.

Aunt Evelyn lit one of the candles, and Tibby knew it was for Esther. Then they both knelt before the statue.

Tibby looked up at the statue. Jesus' arms were outstretched to reveal a bright red heart, wrapped in thorns. His face looked sad and kind, almost like Abraham Lincoln's.

Then she looked at the rows of candles in red glass cups. Almost half of them were flickering with the prayers of people who'd lit them. The rest were dark, waiting for people with more problems and more prayers. It was a lot for anyone — even the Lord God Almighty — to keep track of.

On the way home, Aunt Evelyn stopped by her house to pick up the Sunday newspaper. Tibby got out of the car and helped her snap the heads off some wilting daffodils.

"I suppose I should rent this place out," Aunt Evelyn said, looking around the yard. "I hate to do it, but I don't like to leave it empty every night."

Tibby thought of the Dutch tulips and the photographs in picture frames and the dog door for Lou Grant. This wasn't a beautiful house, but it was a home.

"Why don't you move back here?" Tibby asked.

"Are you trying to get rid of me again? After all we've been through?"

"Maybe," Tibby spoke carefully, "I could live here, too — when Veronica's out of town."

Aunt Evelyn looked at her. "That would be most of the time."

"I know."

The old woman didn't say anything.

"It was just an idea," Tibby said.

"And it was a wonderful idea, Tibby." Aunt Evelyn smiled. "A truly wonderful idea."

Verl was waiting on the front steps when their car pulled into the driveway.

"The doctor thinks Esther is going to be okay," he said. "It'll take a long time, but he thinks she'll make it."

"Thank God," Aunt Evelyn said.

Tibby wanted to take Verl's hand and shake it; she felt so good.

"Will she stay in the hospital?" Aunt Evelyn asked.

Verl shrugged. "The judge says she will, but Brother Ralph is taking it to a higher court."

Aunt Evelyn sighed.

"Where does that leave you?" Tibby asked.

Verl shrugged again. "I don't know."

"You did the right thing," Aunt Evelyn said. "You've got to remember that, Verl. You did the right thing."

"My parents don't think so."

"Parents aren't always right," Tibby said.

After school the next day Aunt Evelyn drove Tibby to the mall, where she spent almost all of her fifty dollars on a present for Esther.

"That's a lot of money to spend on a get-well present," Aunt Evelyn said. "You should save some of it for yourself."

Tibby shook her head. "Esther needs this."

They stopped by the hospital on the way home, but the nurse said only family members could visit Esther.

Tibby was going to leave the present with the nurse when she saw a small, drab-looking woman come through the revolving doors. It was Mrs. Milner.

When she saw Tibby, Mrs. Milner looked away and started walking quickly toward the elevators.

"Don't let her bother you, Tibby." Aunt Evelyn took her hand.

Then Mrs. Milner stopped. She looked back at Tibby and smiled.

Tibby broke away from Aunt Evelyn and practically ran across the lobby. "Mrs. Milner," she said, "I have a present for Esther."

"Oh, honey. I can't take it."

"Why not? It's not a book or anything like that."

"Esther's father wouldn't want her to have a present. Not from you."

"Oh."

Aunt Evelyn came up and put her hand on Tibby's shoulder. "Come on, Tibby," she said. "Let's go home."

Mrs. Milner looked at them. "But *I* want her to have it. Here, give it to me."

Tibby handed her the package. "It's a Barbie doll. And some clothes."

"Oh, honey. She'll be so happy."

"And you don't have to tell her — or Mr. Milner — that it's from me. You can just give it to Esther. And praise His holy name."